Chapter 1

The orange and black butterfly was fluttering easily across the road, right into the path of their oncoming car.

Henny sucked in her breath, bracing herself for the splat. But somehow, miraculously maybe, the butterfly managed to shoot past the deadly windshield to safety.

Henny exhaled noisily.

Her grandmother turned from the passenger seat in front and peered at her over the top of her glasses. "Are you feeling ill?" she asked.

"Hey, Henny, you're not going to puke, are you?" Alex asked.

"Alex!" Grandma said sharply. "*Puke* is a foul word."

"Well, then, Henny, don't" — Alex made a retching sound — "on me."

"Alex!"

"I'm okay, Grandma," Henny said.

"Good." Grandma turned face front.

"Are we there yet?" another voice asked. It belonged to Celia, the youngest of the Rubin sisters, who'd been fast asleep, her head on Henny's shoulder. "It's hot in here."

"Not yet," said Henny, brushing Celia's damp curls off her forehead. "But I don't think it's much farther."

"Ten point three miles," Grandpa spoke up. It was the first thing he'd said on the entire trip.

Alex let out a groan.

Grandma ignored her. "We'll all have some nice cold lemonade when we get there. And then I'll tell you about the wonderful schedule I have planned for you this summer."

Alex groaned again. Celia yawned. And Henny stifled a sigh. They knew all about Grandma's wonderful schedule:

8–9 A.M.	Breakfast
9–10 A.M.	Morning walk
10–NOON	Project of the day
NOON–1 P.M.	Lunch
1–4 P.M.	Field trip
4–5 P.M.	Free time
5–6 P.M.	Chores
6–7 P.M.	Dinner
7–BEDTIME	Evening entertainment

Grandma stuck to her schedule the way a bluebottle sticks to fly paper—and she expected the girls to stick to it, too, whether they wanted to or not.

And this time, we're here for six whole weeks instead of just one, like usual, Henny thought.

"That's not fair!" Alex had complained when their parents had told them about it. "Just because you're going to look for some old junk in Mexico, we're stuck staying with Grandma and Grandpa!"

"Now, Alex, you know perfectly well it's not old junk we're looking for: It's valuable artifacts."

"It always looks like old junk to me."

"Mommy, why can't we go with you?" Celia had asked.

"Well, sweetie, we're going to be traveling around a lot and living in rough conditions you wouldn't like."

"I would—better than Grandma and Grandpa's," said Alex.

"Me, too," said Celia.

"I don't know what you two are complaining about. Your grandparents have a big house with a lovely garden. The air's fresh there. The streets are clean. And there's lots for you to do."

"But not what we want to do," Alex said.

"Henny, talk some sense into your sisters, will you?" said their dad. He said that often. He didn't know that Henny agreed with Alex, but that she also knew it was a waste of time to argue with her parents once they'd made up their minds about something.

"Come on. Let's go to my room," Henny had said, ushering Alex and Celia out.

"We really are stuck, aren't we?" Alex said.

"We're stuck," said Henny.

"What are we going to do, then?" asked Celia.

"We're going to make the best of it," Henny answered in her most grown-up voice.

"Oh, brother," said Celia.

Alex said something worse.

Then they'd grimly begun to pack.

"Here we are," Grandma said, bringing Henny back to the present. They were driving up the street to the pretty white house Grandma and Grandpa Geffen owned.

"Who's that, Grandma?" Celia asked, pointing at the tall, thin woman walking up her grandparents' driveway.

"She's twenty minutes early," Grandma answered, looking at her watch. "Well, never mind." She waved at the woman and said to Celia, "That's Mrs. Lattislaw. She's a member of the Do-Our-Part Club, like me. She's going to help us make yarn dolls. That will be our project for the day."

"Yarn dolls," Alex grumbled. "I want to play ball."

"Me, too," Celia piped up.

And I want to sit in the garden and read, thought Henny.

But Grandma said firmly, "We're going to sell these dolls at the Gastonville Bazaar. The money's for charity. Remember, girls, we must all do our part."

Without thinking, Henny mouthed the words along with her. Celia saw her do it and laughed.

"What's funny, Celia?" Grandma asked.

"Nothing," Celia answered, putting her hand over her mouth.

Grandma frowned slightly, then went on. "We should be able to make quite a few dolls today. Then we can have lunch and a walk in the park. Not too long a walk: You'll need at least forty minutes to unpack. After dinner we're having a real treat. April Daley is giving a concert tonight in the Town Hall."

"Isn't she the lady with the big bosoms and the funny-looking guitar we saw last year?" Alex asked.

"That wasn't a guitar, Alex," Grandma said, ignoring the reference to the performer's anatomy. "It was a dulcimer. And, yes, we did hear her last year. She was delightful."

"She was boring," said Alex, as Grandpa pulled the car smoothly to a stop in the driveway.

"Alex—" Grandma began.

But just then Mrs. Lattislaw peered into the car window. "I see you've brought me a whole carload of help, Stella."

"Yes, indeed," Grandma said brightly. "All right, girls, bring your bags inside. I'll pour the lemonade, and then we can get right to work."

Alex let out another groan.

Celia laughed again.

And Henny, stifling another sigh, said to herself, Making the best of it is going to be harder work than I thought.

Chapter 2

W here are you going, Alex?"

"Shhh."

Henny turned over on her back and forced open her eyelids. She had to blink a few times until she was able to focus on the scene in front of her. The soft, pinkish gray light filtering through the curtains in their bedroom told her it was almost dawn. Celia, in her pj's, was sitting up in the bed next to hers. Alex, dressed in jeans and a T-shirt, was standing by the door, her baseball glove in her hand.

"What's going on?" Henny croaked out, her voice raspy with sleep.

"Will you two be quiet?" Alex said in a loud whisper. "Sheesh. If it isn't Grandma, it's you two. A person can't do anything by herself around here."

There was a pause, and then she said, "I'm going to play baseball, that's what."

"At six o'clock in the morning?" Henny said, knowing she sounded just like her father and wishing she didn't.

Alex gave a sigh, sat down at the foot of Celia's bed, and looked at both of her sisters. "Okay, remember when we went strawberry picking the other day?"

Henny nodded. How could she forget? There had been a lot of bees in the strawberry field. Celia had gotten stung by one, and her thumb had hurt a lot. Grandma had had to take her into the strawberry farmer's house to treat it. Henny'd gone along to comfort her.

"Well, while you were getting your bee bite taken care of, I met this kid named Timmy. He's the farmer's kid and he's on the Little League team. He told me they have batting practice at nine every morning, but that he gets up real early and that I could come over and toss a few with him before practice starts. He said his mom would give me breakfast. But Grandma gets up at seven, and once she's up, forget it. I'll never be able to play ball, and you know why."

Henny knew. They'd been there just three days, and already they'd gone to two concerts, one sing-a-long, a museum, a hike, and a rummage sale. They'd made yarn dolls, baked brownies, and picked strawberries. Some of the things had been pleasant; some had been boring. And a few of them could've been a lot of fun if Grandma hadn't insisted on when and how and even why they were doing them. Like the berry picking, for instance. Henny'd always enjoyed picking strawberries. It was fun to pluck the juicy fruit slowly, popping one berry in your mouth for every two in the basket. Celia liked doing it, too. And even Alex said it was okay. But when they got to the farm, Grandma told them to work quickly and not eat any berries because they had to fill a lot of pints so the Do-Our-Part Club (which she was running for president of) could make strawberry shortcake for the senior citizens at the Autumn Age Center.

Henny wondered if Grandma was really going to be able to keep up her schedule for five and a half more weeks and was afraid she probably could. "But Grandma will be worried about you. Are you going to leave her a note?" she said to Alex, and thought, There I go again, sounding like Dad.

Alex rolled her eyes. "Yes, I'm going to leave her a note," she mimicked. "It's right here." She pulled a crumpled piece of paper out of her jeans.

"Okay," Henny said, embarrassed. "Well, have a good time."

"Can I come, too?" Celia said, crawling out of bed.

"No. You go back to sleep."

"But I'm not sleepy anymore."

"Well, *pretend* you're sleepy, will ya, so I can get out of here before Grandma wakes —"

Suddenly, from down the hall, a door opened, and

the three girls heard footsteps heading toward their room.

"Too late," said Celia, crawling back under the covers.

Alex dived under her blanket, baseball glove and all, and slammed a pillow over her head.

Henny lay back down and peered at the door through half-closed eyes.

It opened softly and Grandma's head appeared. She glanced around the room with a puzzled expression. Then she quietly shut the door. The girls heard her footsteps pad off, not back to her room, but in the direction of the kitchen.

"She's gone," said Celia.

"Yeah. But I'm not," said Alex, throwing off her pillow. "No thanks to you."

Nobody said anything else for a long time.

"Is Alex still mad at us?" Celia whispered.

"I don't think it's us she's really mad at," Henny whispered back.

They watched Alex charge ahead of them through the door that Grandpa was holding open for them. Grandma shook her head at Alex's behavior. They were all returning from the library, where they'd heard a dull lecture about local insect life. Well, actually the talk wasn't that dull, thought Henny, who liked learning things about all kinds of creatures, but the speaker was — a middle-aged man with watery blue eyes and a monotone voice. Alex had groaned and fidgeted so much the whole time that Grandma escorted them out before the question-and-answer section began.

"I'm going to have a little chat with Alex," Grandma said. "Why don't you two girls go out into the garden and look at how the roses are doing."

The garden! Henny and Celia looked at each other, their eyes brightening. They went at once, Celia skipping ahead of Henny, who had to stop herself from breaking into a run.

The garden was large and quite remarkable. A wide path cut through it, disclosing colorful surprises at every turn. Here was a clump of bright blue bellflowers. There was a bunch of brilliant orange flowers Grandma called butterfly weed because they attracted so many butterflies. In the back were tall delphiniums and hollyhocks. Clematis draped around a trellis. And smack in the center of the path was a brass-faced sundial.

"Let's sit there," Celia said, pointing to the white wrought-iron bench tucked in a corner near the roses. There were two chairs there, too, but the bench was better because from it you could look out over the garden and pretend you were in an enchanted place.

They plunked themselves down and were quiet a long while, enjoying the view. Henny noticed a praying mantis and pointed it out to Celia.

"Ugh!" Celia said. "Shoo!"

The mantis walked slowly away.

"Do you think Grandma's mad at Alex?" Celia asked.

"Do you?" asked Henny.

"Yep." Celia paused, then said, "Is Alex mad at Grandma?"

"She's mad at what Grandma does."

"Alex gets mad a lot. But you don't," Celia said. She stood up and a large insect flew over her head, skimming right through her hair. She ducked behind the bench. "Hey!" she said, brushing at her curls. "What was that?"

"That was a dragonfly."

"A dragonfly? Oooh, I bet its bite is worse than a bee's."

"Uh-uh. A dragonfly doesn't bite. At least not little girls."

"How about little boys?"

Henny laughed. "Not them, either. It just bites other bugs. It's got a big appetite."

Celia came out from behind the bench. "I bet it can get a full stomach around here."

Henny laughed again. "I bet you're right."

Celia went over to a rosebush. "Look at this bug. What's this one, Henny? It's kind of pretty."

Henny got up to see what Celia was looking at. The bug was about the size of her dad's thumbnail, with a hard black shell that had dull yellow bands on the edges. At first Henny couldn't recall ever seeing one like it. "I don't know," she said. "Maybe some kind of . . ." Then she remembered two slides the man with the monotonous voice had shown them in the library. The first was a picture, taken at twilight, of a garden lit up by fireflies. "Most people have seen fireflies at night," the lecturer had said. "But not as many people would recognize a firefly in the daytime. Here's what it looks like." And he showed the next slide, of a bug perched on a patch of grass in the sunlight. It was the same bug she and Celia were staring at.

"A lightning bug!" Henny said. "You know, like the ones we saw at the Fourth of July picnic last year." Her voice trailed off as she realized she'd made a mistake in mentioning the picnic. It was one of Celia's favorite things, and she didn't need to be reminded of it, since this year they were going to miss it.

Celia's eyes got wide and teary. "I want to go on the picnic this year. Can we?"

"Oh, Celia, you know we can't. We're here, not home."

"We can go home."

"No, we can't. And even if we could, Mom and Dad wouldn't be there, anyway."

"I'm mad at Mom and Dad," Celia said, running back to the bench, sitting down hard, sticking out her lower lip and crossing her arms over her chest.

She looked so much like Alex that Henny felt like laughing at her. But she knew that Celia really was upset.

"You know, that firefly, that lightning bug over there, isn't your *average* lightning bug." When Celia didn't respond, Henny went on, "No, sirree. That firefly is none other than"—she paused dramatically—"Lightey the Lightning Bug."

Celia didn't say anything, but Henny saw her eyes dart toward the rose where the firefly was still nestled.

"That's right — Lightey, the Top Bug in this whole garden." She paused again.

This time, she was rewarded by Celia's turning toward her. "How come? How come he's Top Bug?" Celia asked.

"Because . . . because he's got the most brains, the biggest heart, and . . . and the brightest light of any bug around."

"Oh," said Celia.

"The thing is, though, he's also stubborn and boastful, and even though he's Top Bug, not all the other bugs like him. Lightey's got a terrible temper, too. In fact, that's what got him into big trouble just the other day."

By now, Celia had forgotten about her own burst of bad temper. "What happened?" she asked eagerly.

"Well —" Abruptly, Henny stopped talking. The back door of the house had just closed with a bang. Henny waited for Grandma's gray head to appear over the rosebushes.

But, instead, it was a baseball cap she saw, then Alex's face, looking a little less angry and a little more tired.

"Did you get yelled at?" Celia asked her.

"Grandma never yells," Alex grumbled.

"What did she do, then?"

"She told me just because I missed Mom and Dad was no reason to spoil everyone else's fun."

"But we're not having fun," Celia said.

"I tried to tell Grandma that, but she wouldn't believe me. Anyway, she's making dinner now. We're going to eat earlier today. She said I should go out into the garden with you two until she's finished. I think she's had enough of me today."

"You mean we get to stay here awhile and do *nothing*? No chores?" Henny asked.

"Yeah. Can you believe it?"

"Goody!" said Celia. "Then Henny can tell us what happened to Lightey. Look, Henny, Lightey's gone!"

Henny turned to the rosebush. "He must've flown away. Don't worry. He hasn't gone far. This is his garden."

"What are you two talking about?" demanded Alex.

Henny hesitated. She didn't often tell stories to Alex, because Alex never seemed to be interested. But before she could say anything at all, Celia answered for her, "He's a lightning bug and he's Top Bug of this garden because he's smart and nice and he's got a bright light. But he's got a bad temper and it got him into trouble. Just like you."

Henny wondered if Alex was about to turn her temper against Celia. But Alex just laughed. "Oh, yeah? What kind of trouble?" She turned to Henny. Celia did, too.

Henny looked from one to the other. Then she said, "Okay, I'll tell you."

"But you have to sit down and be quiet," Alex finished for her.

Henny gave her a warning look.

"Okay, okay. I'm sorry. Go on. Tell us."

"All right." Henny settled herself on a chair across from the bench, paused a moment, and began:

o o o

It was early morning, time for lightning bugs to be sleeping. Lightey raised his hard yellow and black body tiredly from the leaf on which he'd been lying. Something had awakened him—a very loud crunching. He squinted first at the sun, then at a neighboring flower. A dark pink Japanese beetle was busily at work getting her breakfast. Lightey had gone to bed in a bad mood. Last night he'd had to sit through a long, boring concert by the Cricket Carolers. And now this noisy beetle had made him wake up in a bad mood, too.

"Hey, find another flower," he snapped.

"I beg your pardon?" the beetle replied.

"I happen to like looking at that flower, if you don't mind, so you just fly off to another one."

"This leaf happens to be very tasty, and I've come quite a distance."

"It's obvious you don't know the rules. Rule Number 1: Let sleeping fireflies lie. Rule Number 2: Don't destroy your host's property."

"I'm simply enjoying a well-earned meal," the beetle interrupted.

"Rule Number 3: Don't talk back to your wisers. Now move it."

The beetle was so annoyed her antennae were

quivering, but she slowly finished off the bit of green she had been chewing before she said a word. Then she let Lightey have it. "Just who do you think you are, a big shot praying mantis? You're a miserable beetle just like I am. Yes, you are."

o o o

"She's wrong. Lightey's a firefly," Celia interrupted.

Henny grinned. Celia was defending Lightey already. "No, she's right. You see, a firefly is a kind of beetle. But Lightey, who's a leader among bugs, thinks he's better than your average beetle any day."

o o o

So, Henny continued, he got upset. So upset that he began to glow, even though it was daytime. "Listen, you garden pest, we may both be beetles, but that's where the resemblance ends. I am a lightning bug, a firefly, a glowworm. Songs and plays have been named after me. Legends have been written about me. Name me one song about a Japanese beetle!"

"What a snob." The beetle yawned and flew off.

"Come back here, you. I haven't finished yet," Lightey yelled.

But the beetle was gone.

For the rest of the day, Lightey could hardly sleep. He flitted and fretted and his light flickered on and off all day long. Night came, and the fireflies gathered at Lightey's leaf for a big meeting about the light show for the Fly, Flutter, Creep, and Crawl Summer Festival.

"We're all here," said Lightey's good friend Jerome.

"All right," groaned Lightey, exhausted from his sleepless day. "Get in your places and we'll practice your parts." Quickly, the lightning bugs got into position. "Now, the first row flashes like this."

Then, tragedy struck.

o   o   o

"Uh-oh," said Celia.

"That's right," said Henny.

o   o   o

Lightey's light wouldn't flash. It wouldn't even turn on! He tried again. No luck. He tried harder and harder. Then he became frightened.

"What's happening?" the bugs began to whisper.

"What's the matter, Lightey?" Jerome asked in a low voice.

"Something's wrong with my light. You better take over for now." And off flew Lightey, trying all the while to glow. "How can I face anyone?" he cried. He found a little hole in the wall of the Geffens' house and crawled into it.

The next day, the word was out all over the garden: Lightey's light had gone out. "He was getting to be too much of a big shot, anyway," a few jealous bugs said.

But Lightey's friends were worried.

"What are we going to do about the show?"

Franny the Young Firefly said.

"Never mind the show. What about poor Lightey?" Drusilla the Fruitfly cried. "Does anyone know where he is?"

"No, but we'll find him," beautiful Twinky the Monarch Butterfly and Jerome said together. And they searched and searched, but they couldn't find him at all.

In the meantime, Lightey lay in his hole, too embarrassed to come out. Without my light, I'm nothing, he thought, feeling terribly sorry for himself. He stayed there for three days while Jerome, Twinky, Drusilla, Franny, and the other bugs kept searching.

"I hope he isn't . . . dead," Drusilla said, and began to cry.

"Of course he's not," Twinky snapped. "Stop talking like that."

But the fireflies were growing restless without their leader, and Jerome was terribly tired from trying to keep order and hold rehearsals, while staying up all day to look for Lightey.

Finally, George the Centipede happened to be climbing the wall, and he noticed the little hole. A curious creature who spoke only in rhymes, he peeked in and saw a still, dark shape. "Tell me true, who are you?" he said.

There was no answer.

"Did you hear what I said, or are you dead?"

"It's Lightey," he croaked feebly.

"My heavens, what luck! Thought you were a dead duck." And George quickly called Twinky,

Jerome, Franny, and Drusilla.

"Lightey!" they all yelled. "Why have you been hiding?"

"No one wants a lightning bug with no light," he mumbled.

"You're too proud," Jerome said. "You don't trust bugs to like you for what you are!"

"And you're dumb," said Twinky. "You haven't done anything to get your light fixed. Off to Ms. Mantis with you."

o   o   o

"Is Ms. Mantis that scary bug we saw before?" Celia interrupted.

"Uh-huh," said Henny.

"You should have seen her, Alex. She — "

"Shhh," Alex said. "Go on, Henny."

Henny, a little surprised at Alex's interest, raised her eyebrows and did.

o   o   o

Then Twinky added, "Can you fly?"

"I think so. I'm just a bit stiff from lying here so long."

Millicent Ladybug, Ms. Mantis's assistant, greeted them. "Good afternoon. Ms. Mantis, chemist, physician, and Doctor of Philosophy, will be with you shortly." She said the same thing to everybody, even though everybody knew who Ms. Mantis was. "Who is the patient?"

"I am," said Lightey, meekly.

Then out came Ms. Mantis, saying, "Millicent, order some new stingers for the wasps, will you? Oh, hello. Well, well, it's Lightey. I understand that you were missing."

"Yes," he whispered.

"What seems to be the trouble?" Ms. Mantis asked, although she already knew the answer.

"I've lost my light," he mumbled.

"Speak up. I couldn't hear you."

"I said I've lost my light."

"Hmmm. Very interesting. Were you perhaps very upset, causing a blowout? Or did you use it during the daytime?"

Lightey remembered the argument with the Japanese beetle and how he had gotten so angry that he had glowed on and off all day long. "Both," he answered, very, very embarrassed.

"I see." She paused for a long time. Lightey's antennae drooped in shame.

"Can he be helped?" Drusilla cried.

"Stop crying at once," Ms. Mantis ordered, and Drusilla did. "Yes, of course he can. As a physician and chemist, I will give you a new dose of glow powder, to use as directed. And as a Doctor of Philosophy, I will give you a piece of advice: Next time, watch your temper, or you're likely to blow a fuse, in a manner of speaking. By the way, what were you angry about, if I may ask?"

"A Japanese beetle was eating a flower near me," Lightey said slowly.

"You should have sent her to me."

"What would you have said?" Franny asked curiously.

"Said? Nothing at all. I would have eaten her."

o   o   o

"Ugh!" shouted Celia.

Alex laughed.

Henny ignored them both and went on:

o   o   o

"That Ms. Mantis is really something," Twinky said, after they'd left her place. "Eaten her. Oh, my!"

"Yeah, well, she's tough, all right. I'm sure glad I got my light back, though." And even though it was daytime, Lightey flashed on his light.

All the bugs recognized it at once and surrounded Lightey. "Hooray, hooray! He's back," they cheered.

"Lightey, remember what Ms. Mantis said about glowing during the day," Twinky said.

And all together, Twinky, Jerome, Franny, and Drusilla yelled, "Now, turn off that light!"

"Oops," said Lightey, and he did.

o   o   o

For a long moment after Henny finished, no one spoke. Then Celia said, "That was a good story. My favorite part was when Lightey got his light back. What was your favorite part, Alex?"

Alex, who'd been quiet during the story, said, "I didn't have a favorite part. But I would've if Ms.

Mantis had actually eaten the Japanese beetle."

"Ugh! Alex Rubin, you're disgusting!"

Alex laughed again.

Suddenly, a cowbell rang loudly. "Dinner!" Grandma shouted from the back door.

"Moo!" answered Alex.

This time, both she and Celia laughed together. Then Celia skipped away toward the house.

Henny stood up and started to follow, but Alex touched her arm. "That was a pretty good story, Henny," Alex said.

Henny guessed Alex wasn't mad anymore. "Thanks," she said.

But then Alex surprised her even more than she had before. "Maybe you could tell us another one sometime."

"Sure," Henny said. "Maybe I could."

Alex smiled and punched her lightly on the shoulder.

Side by side, they sauntered toward the house.

Chapter 3

It was the Fourth of July, and Alex had disappeared.

Henny didn't have any trouble finding her. She was in a clearing in the park not more than forty yards from where the Do-Our-Part Club picnic was taking place. "Hey, Alex," Henny said. "Want me to pitch a few balls?"

"You can't pitch for beans," Alex said, slashing her bat through the low-hanging leaves of an oak tree.

"Then you pitch and I'll hit."

"You hit even worse than you pitch." Slash, slash, slash went Alex's bat again. Then she threw the bat down. It bounced off a rock with a thunk and narrowly missed striking her ankle. She kicked it aside. "Grandma stinks!" she growled. "I won that race.

You saw me. I won it, didn't I?"

"Yes, you did." Henny had to agree.

"So it isn't fair! You don't give a prize to the loser. Besides, I don't even care about the prizes. Those dopey kids can have all my prizes — as long as they know *I* won."

Henny nodded. She didn't care about winning the way Alex did, and she did think it was sort of unfair for her sister to get all the prizes. But she also thought that pretending someone hadn't won a race when she had wasn't playing by the rules.

"This picnic stinks, too," Alex said, throwing herself on a patch of grass. "I wish it would rain."

Henny was inclined to agree. When Grandma had told her about the picnic yesterday, she thought it might be fun. Grandpa was going to cook his famous chili dogs. Grandma said there'd be other kids and they'd have games with prizes. "We're having a Fourth of July picnic after all," she told Celia, who got very excited. They both pictured a nice day in the park, running around, doing whatever they wanted to do.

But it hadn't turned out that way. First of all, Grandma and her Do-Our-Part Club had rounded up a bunch of city kids who were getting to spend a summer in the country, and they expected Henny and her sisters to hang around with them the whole time. Then, one of the kids knocked over the bowl with Grandpa's chili sauce. Grandpa tried to make a joke about having "hot hot dogs instead of chili ones," but nobody laughed. Next, Grandma handed out printed schedules of games and activities, which everyone had to follow. Henny didn't mind the kids or the games, but she wanted some time to be alone with her sisters or by herself, and she hadn't gotten any—until now.

Henny knew she and Alex were supposed to rejoin the others, who were busy playing Simon Says. Instead, with a wiggle of her eyebrows, she said, "Want to do a rain dance?"

"A what?" asked Alex.

"A rain dance. To make the rain come."

"How do you do that?" Alex asked, uncertain as to whether or not she really believed there was such a thing.

"Well, first you have to concentrate real hard. And while you're concentrating, you move your feet like this." Henny shuffled back and forth in a circle. "And you move your hands like this. . . . And you keep concentrating until in your mind you see big, black clouds gathering, blotting out the sun."

Alex got up and started to imitate Henny.

"That's it. Now close your eyes and see the clouds. Soon, you hear thunder rumbling. There's a flash of lightning! Move faster. Faster."

Alex did.

"The rain is beginning to fall. Plink, plink. Just a few fat drops at first. Plink, plunk. Then a few more. Plinkety, plinkety, plinkety."

Both girls shuffled faster.

"And more. Rattattatta. Now it's pouring, pouring—"

"Pouring!" yelled Alex, spinning around.

"What're you doing?" Celia said.

Henny let out a yelp of surprise. Alex was so startled she spun into a tree and fell down. "Owww," she said. "Why'd you sneak up on us like that, dummy?"

"I wasn't sneaking. Grandma told me to find Henny, who was supposed to be finding you. Anyway, what were you doing?"

"A rain dance," Alex said.

"To make it rain?" asked Celia, looking from Alex to Henny.

Henny nodded a bit sheepishly. Celia was probably having a good time, and it wasn't fair to spoil it for her.

"Oh, good. Then we can go home."

"You want to leave, too?" Henny asked.

"Yes. This big bratty kid kept kicking me the whole time we played Simon Says. He stole my chocolate-chip cookies, too."

She sat down on the ground next to Alex.

They were all quiet a minute.

"It's strange that we want it to rain on a picnic, isn't it?" said Henny. "Remember the year it really did rain on the Fourth of July and we were all mad?"

"Uh-huh," Alex said.

"I don't remember," said Celia.

"You were just a baby then," said Alex.

"We could've used Lightey's help then," said Henny.

"Lightey? How could he have helped?" asked Celia.

"Why, Lightey once saved the day at a picnic for a family who used to live here."

"Yeah? How'd he do that?" asked Alex.

"You really want to know?"

"Yes," said both Alex and Celia together.

"Okay. Then I'll tell you the story of Lightey and the picnic."

o   o   o

It was morning again, and Lightey, as usual, was fast asleep. So fast asleep that he hardly heard a voice say, "Wake up."

"Huhhh?" he groaned, and crawled under his leaf.

"I said wake up!"

"Coming, Mother," said Lightey.

"I'm not your mother."

"What's going on?" Lightey grunted and looked up.

Little Gloria the Garden Spider was standing in front of him. "Gloria, what do you want?" he asked.

"For goodness sake, you told me to wake you up this morning," the spider said, sounding a bit annoyed. "Something about a picnic, you said."

"Picnic! Gee, thanks, Gloria. I nearly forgot. By

the way, don't mention this to anyone. We don't want too much of a crowd, you know."

"Who are you going with?"

"Uh, just a few friends."

"Oh, I see," sniffed Gloria, and started to crawl away.

"I'm not insulting you, Gloria. It's the Lubins."

"The Lubins!" Gloria turned back. "Why didn't you say so? They have plenty of room in their car."

"Yeah, but, well, I don't want to hurt your feelings, but, well, uh, you see, I don't think they'd much like a spider along."

"Humph. Don't ask me for any more favors," Gloria snapped, and quickly rushed off.

"Gloria, I don't mind spiders. The Lubins, see, they don't . . . Aw, phooey, she's too sensitive," Lightey said. "I hope she doesn't spill the beans." Then he concentrated on how to sneak into the Lubins' car, unnoticed by them and by his fellow bugs.

"What are you doing up so early?" a voice suddenly boomed into his antenna.

"Yahhh!" Lightey jumped. "Oh, Morris, you scared me," he said to a long, pink earthworm, who was something of a comedian.

"Ha, ha," Morris said, and did a complete roll. "The worm has turned. Ha, ha." He giggled.

"Ha, ha, very funny," Lightey answered sarcastically.

"So what are you doing?" Morris asked.

"Oh, uh, I'm planning my speech for the Speaker of the House and Garden contest."

"The Speaker of the House and Garden contest isn't for another two months."

"It never hurts to plan ahead." Lightey was a bad liar.

"Oh, well, for a minute I thought you were going on the Lubins' picnic."

"Picnic!" Lightey squeaked. "Whatever gave you that idea?"

"Nothing. I've just seen you hanging around their window every evening while they were planning it, that's all."

"Nonsense. I've just—"

"You better hurry. They'll be leaving soon."

Lightey was speechless.

"And don't worry. I won't tell anyone. Worm's the word." If Morris could have winked, he would have. "See you later," he said, and off he wriggled.

If he doesn't tell anyone, I'll be a bumblebee's uncle, thought Lightey. All the Lubins need is a crowd of bugs at their picnic. There'll be enough ants as it is. Anyway, I hope they haven't left yet. Flexing his wings, he flew toward the window and nearly collided with Twinky the Monarch Butterfly.

"Lightey, what on earth are you doing up at this hour?" she asked, as she hovered gracefully.

Here we go again, he thought. But, cheerfully, he said, "Oh, hi, Twinky. It's my new program for increasing my glowing power—an extra dose of vitamin D." This is a better lie than my last one, he thought, getting involved with his story. "After all, the sun supplies vitamin D, and it shines ever so bright —"

"Lightey, what are you up to, and why won't you tell me?" Twinky interrupted.

Curses, foiled again, he thought. "Okay, I was just kidding. Look, do you promise you won't tell anyone?"

"Sure. You know you can count on me."

"All right. I'm going on a picnic with the Lubins."

"Ooooh, how terrific! Can I come along?"

Is there no escape, Lightey thought. "Gee, I'd like you to, Twink, but it wouldn't work. I mean, you'd be awfully conspicuous, and they'd probably try to catch you."

She shuddered. "I sure wouldn't like being pinned in a case like my poor Aunt Emily."

"Oh, no, the Lubins would never do that. They're very kind to animals. Even the youngest girl. No, they'd probably try to put you out the car window, to set you free, and that'd mean a long, unnecessary flight back here."

"Oh, I'm used to long flights. After all, I migrate, don't I?"

"Then you need all of your strength. It'd be silly to waste it now. Besides, you'd never make it to the picnic anyway if they put you out."

"Hmmmm, I guess you're right. Well, have a good time and let me know all about it. Who else is going with you?"

"Oh, I'm going alone," Lightey said, trying to sound casual. "You won't mention it to anyone, will you?"

"Alone, huh? As I said before, you can count on me. If there's any trouble — or if you want some company — signal."

"Thanks, Twink," Lightey said, and, happy to stop hovering, he flew on to the window. Oh boy, oh boy, so many delays. I hope I'm not late, he thought.

Mr. Lubin was putting food into a big, old-fashioned picnic basket. "Penny, Allie, Delia, all my pumpkins, let's go!" he called.

Three girls, followed by their neighbor's puppy named Fred-Mabel, ran in. Penny was carrying a red Frisbee and a striped blanket. Allie had a football. And Delia, who was the youngest, was struggling with an umbrella as big as she was.

"Good grief, what's that for?" Mr. Lubin asked.

"It might rain," said Delia.

"Oh, no, it won't. Look how the sun's shining."

"It might sun too hard," Delia answered, and everyone laughed.

Mrs. Lubin, fresh from riding her bicycle, popped into the kitchen.

"Mommy!" yelled the girls as they rushed her out to the car.

Lightey, gleeful that he hadn't missed the picnic, was just about to fly to the car when he heard a low voice next to him.

"Family scene, wholesome and clean/They never

act cross and they never act mean."

"George," Lightey, whirling around, said to the centipede. "Terrific poem — one of your best yet. See you later and we can discuss it."

Before the startled centipede could utter another rhyme, Lightey was gone. He slipped into a nook by the rear window of the Lubins' automobile and sighed.

This is the life, thought Lightey, as he settled down for a comfortable ride. Aren't I clever to slip away like this?

Soon, they reached the park, and they all tumbled out of the car—all except Lightey, that is, who, of course, flew out instead. Mr. Lubin spread out the blanket and opened the picnic basket, and Mrs. Lubin played tug-of-war with Fred-Mabel over the Frisbee. The girls started a game of tag. It was turning out to be just what everyone had wanted — a good, old-fashioned picnic — and they were all so happy they didn't realize that the sun had somehow disappeared.

Lightey perched on a blade of grass. "You ants had better buzz off," he told a little army that had started toward the picnic basket.

"We don't buzz," one ant said nastily.

"Your head will if you don't get lost," Lightey answered bravely.

"You against all of us? Ha! We could carry off a snake if we wanted to," the ant bragged.

"Oh, yeah? Want me to signal a few of *my* friends?"

"Aw, who needs this lousy food, anyway? We can do much better. Come on, ants." And away they all went.

"Why so fast? Ants in your pants?" Lightey called after them. But then he laughed at himself. I sound like that goofy Morris the Earthworm.

Soon, Mr. Lubin began to unpack the food. Out came sandwiches and olives and pickles and potato chips and coleslaw and carrots and peaches and cherries and cookies and lemonade. "What a feast!" yelled Allie, charging at the food. Then, of course, something awful happened. The sun disappeared. The sky got as dark as the inside of a cocoon. The clouds opened up and rained down on the Lubins, on their food, and on Lightey.

"Oh, no," cried Penny.

"The umbrella!" shrieked Delia, and she ran to the car to get it while everyone else tried to gather up or eat the food as quickly as possible. Penny went to help her. Soon, the Lubins were all huddling under the umbrella, looking at the rain and their soggy food and feeling very sad.

"It will stop soon," Mrs. Lubin said, but no one was very convinced.

"I went through all that trouble for this," said Lightey to no one in particular. "And I got up so early, too." Then he stopped. "Hey, I'm busy feeling sorry for myself, and look at the poor Lubins."

"So go and do something about it," a scurrying ant sneered at him.

"I think I just might," Lightey snapped back.

And, in fact, he did have an idea. He began to signal frantically. I hope I don't have another blowout, he thought.

Nearby, a lightning bug named Glimmer saw the signal and flashed it to her friends. Among them was a visiting firefly from a garden near Lightey's. He knew Lightey and he knew Jerome and he rushed to Jerome with the message.

"Holy firefly!" said Jerome, and rounded up all the lightning bugs in the neighborhood. "We've got to help the Lubins. But first we've got to go to Ms. Mantis and get some extra glow powder."

"Hurry up," Franny urged.

Ms. Mantis was eating a louse when the huge band of fireflies arrived. She peered at them sternly. "And what do you all mean, charging at me this time of day?"

Jerome quickly told her.

"Well, in that case, I will be delighted to help."

It was still raining and very dark when Jerome and the other lightning bugs arrived at the picnic spot. "Thank heavens you've come," said Lightey. "Are you all ready? Do you know what we're going to do?"

"We know," said Jerome.

"Okay, then. Come on," Lightey commanded, and all the lightning bugs silently flew under the Lubins' umbrella, where the family was still standing miserably.

"One, two, three," Lightey whispered. And all the fireflies lit up together.

"Look!" cried Delia.

"What is it?" asked Allie.

"Not the sun," said Mrs. Lubin.

"They're lightning bugs!" said Penny.

"So they are. How did they get here?" said Mr. Lubin.

"Maybe the sun sent them." Delia giggled.

"No, it didn't," said Jerome.

"Shut up and glow," ordered Lightey.

Holding up her hands to them, Delia laughed again. "This is the best picnic ever!"

"Speaking of which, how come you never bothered to ask us along?" Jerome asked that evening, when all the fireflies were back in the garden.

"Yeah," added the others.

"Well, I . . . you see . . . you all hate getting up early —"

"Lightey," they all interrupted him, "shut up and glow." And Lightey did.

o   o   o

"Lightey really did save the day," Celia said.

"Uh-huh." Henny nodded.

"Maybe we ought to start a Lightey fan club," joked Alex.

"Ooooh, can I join?" asked Celia.

"Silly, it was just a jo —"

"No. It isn't," Henny interrupted her. "It's . . . it's just what we need."

"Need? For what?"

"For whenever we can get away from Grandma.

Then we'll have a secret meeting of The Lightey Club."

"What'll we do at these secret meetings? Shut up and glow?"

"No, silly," Celia said. "Henny'll tell us more Lightey stories, that's what. Right, Henny?"

"Sure," said Henny. "I can do that."

There was a pause. Then Alex said, "The Lightey Club. Not bad. I'm glad I thought of it."

This time it was Henny who rolled her eyes.

Chapter 4

Days had passed, but The Lightey Club didn't get to meet again.

"We've got to have a meeting this afternoon," Alex said in the girls' room of the library, where Grandma'd taken them for another lecture. This one was called "Gastonville During the Revolutionary War," and not even Henny found it the least bit interesting.

"Then we have to come up with some excuse," Henny said.

"Excuse for what?"

"For why we're not going to the McDonald Inn where George Washington stopped on his way to Valley Forge."

"What'd he stop there for? A cheeseburger and fries?" Celia giggled.

"Ha, ha," sneered Henny. "You're almost as funny as Morris the Earthworm."

"Uh-oh. Look who's in a bad mood for a change," said Alex.

It was true. Henny *was* in a bad mood. Before the lecture began, she'd slipped into the children's section of the library and found a book on lightning bugs. She'd looked through it quickly and discovered all sorts of interesting information. She wished she could spend the afternoon quietly, reading it. But, instead, she had to shove it back on the shelf when Grandma came looking for her and go listen to a boring lecture that made her very sleepy. Maybe a Lightey Club meeting *is* what I need, she thought. "Okay," she said, forcing her mind to clear. "Celia, you've got a stomachache."

"I do?" said Celia.

"Yes. You have to go home and you want Alex and me to keep you company."

"When I have a tummy ache I don't want any company."

Alex groaned. "This is pretend, Celia. You have to pretend you have a tummy ache."

"I'm not good at pretending."

"Then maybe Alex should—" Henny began.

"Not me. Grandma'll never believe I'm sick. She'll know I just want to get out of going. But if you say you're sick, Henny, she'll definitely believe you."

Henny frowned. She didn't think she was good at that sort of pretending, either. But she agreed to do it.

The three sisters left the girls' room and spotted Grandma, who was sitting nearby at a table. A very bent and wrinkled old man was leaning on his cane and talking loudly to her. It seemed to Henny that Grandma looked a bit pale and puffy-eyed.

"You going to have enough of them cupcakes this year?" the man was asking.

"Yes, Mr. Fogerty. We'll have enough."

"I never got mine last year, you know that? I told that Mamie somebody—the one who handed out the cupcakes. She didn't listen to me. I told that Lattislaw dame, too, but she didn't listen to me, either. Are you going to listen to me?"

"I'm listening to you now, Mr. Fogerty."

"I want one with that pink whatchamacallit on it."

"Icing."

"Yeah. That's it. Icing. Pink icing. And sprinkles. You make sure I get one this time, you hear."

"I'll make sure, Mr. Fogerty. I'll put your name on it with the sprinkles," Grandma said firmly.

Henny had the most peculiar feeling that she and her sisters ought to rescue Grandma. She walked over purposefully, followed by Alex and Celia, completely forgetting her "tummy ache" for the moment.

"Hello, girls. This is Mr. Fogerty," Grandma said. "Mr. Fogerty, my granddaughters, Henny, Alex, and Ce—"

Mr. Fogerty cut her off. "Don't like kids. They eat all the cupcakes." He turned around rather quickly for his age and hobbled off.

Grandma shook her head slightly and rubbed her temples.

No one said anything for a moment. Then Alex gave Henny a poke, and Henny remembered what she was supposed to do. She bent over slightly, wrinkling her face. "Grandma, I—"

But Grandma interrupted her. "Girls, I hate to disappoint you, but I'm afraid I have a bad headache. I don't like to have to do this, but, if you don't mind, we'll visit McDonald Inn another day."

"Great!" said Alex. "I mean—"

"No, we don't mind," Henny put in quickly, straightening up.

"Are you sure? I want you girls to have fun while you're here," Grandma said, sounding truly distressed.

"Oh, yes. We'll have fun. Don't worry about us. We'll, uh, *occupy* ourselves." That was a word their father used a lot.

"Thank you. That's very considerate of you, girls," said Grandma. "I'm sure with a little rest I'll be fine for tonight's dance recital."

"What dance recital?" asked Alex.

"The Moldavian Folk Troupe is performing."

"Oh, brother."

Henny poked Alex. "Can you drive all right, Grandma?" she asked.

"Yes, I think so, dear." She led them to the car.

And that's how, a short while later, The Lightey Club came to be sitting comfortably in the garden.

"I wonder when Grandma finds time to work in this garden," Henny mused out loud. She was glad The Lightey Club was meeting, but she was also feeling a bit guilty without knowing exactly why. It didn't seem quite right to be having fun because Grandma was sick. "I'd sort of like to work in it myself."

"Do gardens need a lot of work?" asked Celia.

"You bet. You have to plant and weed and trim and —"

"Get rid of bugs," said Alex.

"Not Lightey?" Celia's voice rose.

"Not Lightey." Henny shook her head.

"Or Twinky?"

"Or Twinky or Jerome or Franny or Morris or Gloria or even Ms. Mantis. They're all good bugs."

Celia nodded. Then she said, "Maybe Grandpa works in it."

Henny looked at her in surprise. "Maybe he does. I never thought of that."

"Let's not talk about Grandma and Grandpa," said Alex impatiently. "Let's talk about Lightey. We're The *Lightey* Club, remember?"

Henny let out a tiny sigh. "Okay."

"What I want to know," Alex said, "is how did Lightey get to be Top Bug of this garden?"

"That's a good question," said Henny. "Let me see. . . . Well, he'd been living here for a while and he was already the leader of the lightning bugs because he was so good at organizing light shows and Meet Your Mate parties and other things. Once, danger threatened the garden."

o o o

The news spread rapidly. Yesterday had been quiet and peaceful, except for the usual forays by birds out for a quick meal. But today — today the Blue Jay was on the loose. A new arrival in the garden, the Blue Jay had struck terror into the hearts of the insect inhabitants.

"Extra, extra," shouted Nick the Fly with an Eye for News. "Hear all about it. Blue Jay Terrorizes Insect Community. Several Bugs Eaten. Others Flee in Panic."

"Oh, my! Oh, my! This is terrible, just terrible," little Drusilla the Fruitfly squeaked as she flew.

"What are we going to do about this menace, Lightey?" Jerome the Firefly asked.

"It's obvious that this bird has no manners. I mean, much as we hate it, we expect birds to go after a few bugs — that's their nature. But this bird is making a regular pig of himself. He must be talked to."

"Okay, but who's gonna do it? He might try to eat us. In the daytime we fireflies may look delicious to him."

"True. The answer is to discover who the monster won't eat and send them to deal with him."

"I thought you knew all about the tastes of birds," Jerome said.

"I do," Lightey bluffed, unwilling to be caught in a lie. "I just don't know who'd agree to approach the beast."

So Lightey and Jerome settled down to think about the problem. And as they did, they heard an enormous buzz approaching. Then the source of the buzz appeared—a group of flies racing to get out of reach of the grasping beak of the Blue Jay. Dismayed, Lightey and Jerome watched him snap up two, then three, then five flies all at once.

"Tasty little snack," the Jay muttered as he soared past in an effortless pursuit of the flies. Lightey and Jerome looked at each other in horror.

In the wake of the massacre, Nick flew by, shouting, "Extra, extra! Blue Jay Slays Ten."

"Hey, how can you be so cool about it? They were your fellow flies," said Lightey.

"I'm a reporter. It's part of my job to be cool and give the facts, just the facts. Extra, extra! House Sparrow Harasses Honeybee. Extra, extra! Honeybee Harasses House Sparrow." And off he went to spy more news.

"I wonder who won," said Jerome, after a silence.

"Who won?" Lightey asked.

"The honeybee or the house sparrow."

"Oh, brother," Lightey snapped. "We've got more important things to worry about."

"I was just wondering."

"Well, wonder about how to stop the Blue Jay instead, okay?"

"Keep out of the way of the nasty Blue Jay. If he comes in sight, you'd better take flight. Or if you can't, then crawl. That's all," said a melancholy voice.

"George!" Lightey and Jerome yelled at once, startling the centipede poet.

"George, old pal, it's been a long time. How are you?" Lightey gushed.

"You saw me yesterday. I think I'm still okay. Except for this Blue Jay."

"Yeah. Funny you should mention him. I thought I'd talk to you about that, you being a poet and a bug of superior intelligence and sensitivity and all that."

George didn't reply. Jerome gave Lightey an encouraging look.

"Yeah, well, it's like this, George. Uh . . . you see . . . how would you like to be of great service to all of us in the bug community?"

"I ask of you what I'd have to do."

"Do? Oh, nothing much. Just talk to someone about something."

"On the spot—who and what?"

"Uh . . . just the Blue Jay."

"You must be nuts! He'd eat me!" George yelled, so upset that he forgot to rhyme, and off he scurried.

"You really are an expert on bird tastes," Jerome said sarcastically.

"Centipedes slipped my mind," Lightey grunted.

"Extra, extra! Grackle Grabs Garden Spider."

"It wasn't Gloria, I hope," Lightey asked, worried.

"Nope. Her distant cousin," Nick answered. "Extra, extra! Blue Jay Rests after Hunt."

"Well, it won't do to ask Gloria. Birds obviously eat spiders." Jerome frowned.

"Listen, you go around and find out where the creep sleeps, and I'll collect some volunteers," Lightey said. "Meet you here later."

"Okay." Jerome took off.

Alone, Lightey sighed and tried to figure out which bugs wouldn't get devoured and which would be brave enough to face the constantly hungry jay.

"Add a little sparkle to your life," a low voice boomed. "A little glow."

"Arrggh! Cut it out, Morris!" Lightey shouted at the jolly earthworm.

"Bet you thought I was that jay. Ha, ha. A jay a day keeps the doctor away — 'cause you're dead. Ha, ha. Get it?"

"This is no time for jokes." Lightey was irritated. But then he suddenly glowed. "Morris, how would you like to be a hero? With your great sense of humor and all, I know you could do it."

"Do what? Do what? Do tell. Do tell."

"It's really simple. All you have to do is talk to the jay."

"Lightey, I thought you had more smarts than that. I may be hard for you to swallow, but I'm filet mignon to a jay. The early bird catches the you-know-what."

"Yeah, sorry. I forgot about that."

"One bite, and me and me would be twins. Two Morrises. How about that?"

"Okay, you made your point."

"Tell you what, though. I think I can suggest someone."

"Who? Who?" Lightey asked excitedly.

"Hold on a minute. I won't make you worm it out of me. Ha, ha. It's Twinky."

"Twinky! You expect me to send a beautiful butterfly to that bully? Any bug is a temptation to a jay, but that's ridiculous. It's sending her to certain death."

"Boy, you don't know much, do you?"

"Why you . . . you . . ." Lightey sputtered.

"No offense, no offense. Ha, ha. Let me explain. Most butterflies may be tempting morsels, but not monarchs. In plain English, to birds they taste lousy. Something they give off, I suppose."

"If you're kidding me, Morris — "

"I kid you not, kid. Ask Twinky. In fact, here she comes."

And, sure enough, the graceful and gorgeous butterfly fluttered up to them. "Gee, everyone's awake. That jay is causing quite a stir," she said, unruffled.

"You don't seem very nervous," Lightey said.

"No, I'm not worried about myself — just about my friends. Birds don't like my taste."

"I told you so," Morris said with a wriggle.

So Lightey told Twinky his idea.

"Sure, I'll go," the butterfly said, "but I can't promise much."

"Extra, extra! B.J. on the Loose Again. Crushes Caterpillar."

"As I was about to say, he seems a pretty stubborn fellow," Twinky added.

"Well, I don't think you should go alone. Can you think of anyone else?"

Just then, Jerome returned. "Horrible! I saw it with my own eyes. That poor caterpillar."

And everyone *tsk*ed. Then they told Jerome about Twinky.

"Well," he said. "Ms. Mantis said I should tell you to meet at her place. She has a plan, too."

So off they all flew (or wriggled) to Ms. Mantis's.

"Ms. Mantis will see you in a moment," Millicent Ladybug, her assistant, said coolly. She'd never liked Lightey—she thought he was rude and ill-bred—but she did respect him. "This is about that terrible jay business, is it not?"

"Yeah," answered Lightey curtly. He didn't care much for Millicent, either.

"Good afternoon." Ms. Mantis entered majestically. "We all know we are here on an important matter. The jay must be stopped, but we must handle him carefully."

Everyone listened attentively. Ms. Mantis was a being of superior strength and intelligence, highly respected by every bug in the garden. "Jerome told me your excellent plan, Lightey, and I have decided that Millicent and I will go."

"But . . . eaten," was all Lightey could choke out.

"Don't worry. Millicent isn't favored by birds," she said tactfully. "Ladybugs in general are not. As for myself, I have stood my ground against sparrows and starlings. A jay doesn't frighten me."

"Twinky," Jerome croaked.

"I beg your pardon?" Ms. Mantis asked.

Lightey found his voice and told her about the butterfly.

"Excellent. Three is a good number. Let's go at once."

When they arrived at the jay's favorite perch, to which Jerome had directed them, they found the bird taking his afternoon rest.

"Mr. Jay," spoke Ms. Mantis boldly.

"Who is it, and whaddya want?" he rasped. "Good grief, three bugs — none edible, except maybe the mantis."

Ms. Mantis immediately raised her forelegs so she looked like a boxer.

"Nope, not the mantis, either," he decided.

"Mr. Jay," she began, keeping the boxer pose.

"You don't have to *mister* me," he interrupted. "The name's J.B. Jay. You can call me J.B."

"*Mr.* Jay," she insisted, "this is not a social call. You have been terrorizing our community. We realize that you must feed on insects to live, but you are going too far."

"Come on, toots. I'm a growing jay and I've got a

big appetite. I'd do my mother proud, bless her soul."

"Then why don't you eat those insects that are pests — the ones that destroy beautiful plants. There are plenty of them. Believe me, I know," Millicent said.

"Ladybug — I'll call you Lady for short, okay?"

"No, it is not okay," Millicent huffed.

But the Jay went on. "Lady, I've got varied tastes. I mean, a bird gets bored, too, you know, with the same diet."

"It's not fair," Twinky piped up.

"Fair, schmair. That's nature, Beauty. Now, if you'll excuse me, I'll continue my nap. I was dreaming about my dear mother. A cat got her. A Siamese. Terrible thing. Nobody'd ever write a book about her, but my mother was a saint." He cried a little, a noisy, scratchy sound. Sniffling, he said, "Excuse me. I still haven't gotten over it. See you again, maybe."

"His dear, departed mother, huh?" said Lightey, after Twinky had repeated the conversation word for word. "What a fruit."

"Fruit or no fruit, Ms. Mantis is very upset. She doesn't know what to do next."

"Twinky, my friend, I think I'm beginning to have a brainstorm. Did I ever tell you what the Indonesians believe about fireflies? They believe they're ghosts! I just wonder . . . I'll give it a try!"

That evening, Lightey flew quietly to the jay's perch. He began to dart among the leaves, flashing

in different rhythms, so that his light would be even more flickering and eerie.

"J.B., J.B.," he whispered in a squeaky voice.

"Whaaat? What is it?" said the sleepy jay.

"Wake up, darling."

"A stupid lightning bug." He coughed and went back to sleep.

"J.B., J.B., J.B."

"Whaddya want, bug?" he groaned.

"I am not a bug. I am the spirit of your mother."

"My mother? You don't sound like my mother."

"Heaven has changed my voice. I can even sing now," Lightey boldly added.

"Huh? Is this for real?"

"My son, I have forgiven the cat."

"The cat! No lightning bug would know about that," the jay gasped.

"The Siamese," Lightey said, hoping he wasn't overdoing it.

"Mother!" bawled the jay. "Why have you come?"

"I have come to warn you. It is not safe here. There are many cats."

"Cats!"

"Cats. Siamese cats, calico cats, tabby cats, Manx cats, Persian cats, tortoise-shell cats, Angora cats. Cats." Lightey waited.

"Where should I go, then?"

"To the park. There are no cats there, but there are lots of bugs."

"Mother, I'll leave in the morning."

"You always were a good son. I must go now."

"Wait! Will I see you again?"

"You will if you don't leave," Lightey muttered.

"What?"

"Nothing, dear. I said *perhaps*, if I am allowed to come again. Good-bye now."

"Mother!" And the jay wailed so hard that Lightey felt sorry for him.

Oh, well, he thought, he'll be happy when he remembers that he "saw" his mother again.

"How'd it go?" all the bugs demanded when Lightey returned.

"It worked," Lightey said.

The next morning, the jay was indeed happy, although he wondered if he had dreamed the whole thing. He ate a hearty breakfast of five grasshoppers, two worms (neither Morris, fortunately), and a lot of aphids. Then he left.

"Extra, extra! Jay Eats and Flies," Nick yelled.

"You did it!" Twinky said to Lightey. "You're going to have to make a speech tonight, after we all elect you Top Bug of the garden."

"Yeah?" said Lightey, who'd seen the jay eat breakfast and no longer regretted at all how he'd pretended to be the bird's mother. "I'd be honored."

"You know what else?"

"What?"

"The jay was heard warning the other birds about an abundance of cats here, so a robin and a wood thrush left for the park with him."

"Oh, no," Lightey said. And he and Twinky laughed until they ached.

Chapter 5

Henny couldn't sleep. In the bed next to hers, Celia was snoring lightly. Across the room, Alex was mumbling words Henny couldn't understand. But it wasn't the snoring or the mumbling that was keeping her awake; she was used to her sisters' sleep noises. It was Lightey and his friends. They were darting around in her head, whispering, flickering, bumping her brain. Time to take a nap now, she told them. But they didn't want to listen.

So she got up, glanced around the dark room, tiptoed to the door, and put her ear against it. She couldn't hear a thing, but she knew that Grandma and Grandpa might still be up. They usually watched TV at night. However, the set was downstairs, and it was hard to tell if it was on or off from the girls' bedroom.

Henny decided to risk it. She opened the door as quietly as she could. The hall was dark and silent. She padded down it, pausing at her grandparents' room. Suddenly, she heard Grandma say, "It *is* difficult. I have to come up with so many things for the girls to do so they don't get bored. But they get bored, anyway. I have to be entertaining all the time. And sometimes I just don't feel like it."

Henny leaned closer to the door. Grandma's tone surprised her. She shifted her feet, waiting to hear Grandpa's answer, and the floor creaked loudly. "Oh, no," she whispered, and flattened herself against the wall. But nobody else seemed to hear the noise. She moved off down the hall as quietly as she could, praying the floor wouldn't creak again. She reached the stairs and sneaked down them, avoiding the last step, which she knew squeaked. Then she slipped into the kitchen.

Moonlight was trickling through the window above the sink, dappling the enamel with spots of silver. Henny picked up a glass lying in the drainer, held it up to the moonlight, and looked through. A crystal world, she thought. She put the glass down, went to the back door, and looked out through the small pane of glass. She couldn't see much of the garden, but she could hear crickets chirring from under some bush or flowering plant. She opened the door slowly and carefully, glad that Grandpa had oiled the hinges only yesterday, and stepped out into — Fairyland.

The moon speckled the leaves, and the very gen-

tle breeze blowing through them made the dots dance. But the moon dots weren't as bright as the lights that skipped among them, the green-golden lights belonging to dozens and dozens of flickering fireflies.

"Oh!" Henny exclaimed aloud, without thinking. "How beautiful!"

"Not bad," she could hear Lightey's voice say. "A little more practice and we'll *really* show you something."

There was enough moonlight for Henny to make her way down the path to the wrought-iron bench without knocking against the sundial or pricking herself on the rose thorns. She sat down to watch the fireflies. How long she sat she wasn't sure.

"I wonder what they're saying," she said.

"Can't you tell?" said a voice at her side. "Maybe we need more practice than I thought."

Henny turned her head.

Lightey was there. "We're spelling out H–E–N–N–Y," he said.

"Henny. That's me."

"Of course it is. We've been calling you for hours."

"Why?"

"To take the grand tour."

"The grand tour? What grand tour?"

"Come on. I'll show you." He streaked up in the air.

Henny got up and followed.

Through the garden they went, through the

bushes and the grasses and the flowers and the trees. They passed a nest of sleeping sparrows and a quiet hive of bees. They saw a pale-winged moth on a pale-petaled flower, a bunch of scurrying beetles, a silent, squatting toad. They heard the chirrings and whirrings and leafy rustlings in the night-scented garden, in the night-scented air.

Then the sky changed color.

"Dawn," said Lightey with a yawn. "Time to go to sleep."

"Lightey, don't go," Henny cried.

"Got to. But I'll be back."

"Lightey!" She tried to go with him, but her body felt as heavy as a rock.

"Shhh, upsy-daisy," a voice whispered in her ear.

"Lightey!" Henny called. She opened her eyes halfway. A blurry face was peering into hers.

"Shhh," the deep voice said again. "We don't want to wake anyone up now, do we?"

"Hmmm," Henny said, as strong arms lifted up her leaden body and carried her through the still-dark garden. "Where's Lightey?"

"Somewhere near, I'm sure."

"Oh. That's good. . . ."

The strong arms carried her upstairs and laid her on a soft bed.

"Good-night, Henny," the deep voice whispered.

"Good-night," she said.

In another moment, the arms and voice were gone.

And in the next, Henny's eyes shot open. The

sunlight was hitting her full in the face. Celia was sitting on her bed. "I had the strangest dream," Henny said. "I was in the garden with Lightey."

"Lightey?"

"Yes. Lightey and . . . oh, no!"

"Oh, no, what?" Alex asked sleepily from across the room.

"There was someone else in the garden. And I think it was Grandpa!"

Chapter 6

"Was Grandpa really in the garden with you?" Celia asked.

Henny didn't say anything right away. She was beginning to wonder about the answer. An entire day had passed, and Grandpa hadn't said one word about the episode or given her any winks or funny looks. Neither had Grandma, which meant that either Grandpa hadn't told her or the whole thing had been a dream.

But, then, how did I get up to bed, she asked herself. Did I sleepwalk? No, I remember someone carrying me, and he had Grandpa's voice. But what was Grandpa doing in the garden so early? And how long had he been there? Henny knew that all she had to do to find out was to go and ask Grandpa. But she felt too embarrassed to do it.

"I hope you didn't tell him about Lightey," said Alex. "That's our secret."

Henny still didn't speak. She had a nagging feeling that she *had* said something about Lightey, but she couldn't remember what it was. She hoped it was very little. "I . . ." she began.

"Shhh," warned Alex.

Grandma and Grandpa were walking into the kitchen. Grandpa was carrying a drill, and Grandma was waving a smallish white envelope. "Look, girls," she said. "A letter from your mother and father."

"Oh, goody, goody, goody!" Celia said, jumping up and down.

"It's about time," grumbled Alex. "We've been here for three weeks already, and this is the first letter we've gotten from them."

"This was postmarked a week and a half ago," said Grandpa. "The mail's pretty slow from Chimichihuanga."

"Chimichi-what?"

"Chimichihuanga. That's three thousand, four hundred, and fifty-seven miles from here. It's where your parents are." He walked over to a corner of the room and plugged in the drill.

"What does the letter say?" asked Celia. "Read it to us, Henny."

Using a brass letter opener, Grandma carefully slit the top of the envelope, took out a single sheet of paper, and handed it to Henny to read. Henny appreciated the fact that Grandma hadn't opened and read the letter before she and her sisters had had a chance to. But that's where Grandma's sense of privacy ended. Instead of leaving them alone so they could enjoy it in peace, she was waiting to hear it, too.

"Hurry up, Henny," Celia said.

Henny gave a little sigh. " 'Dear Henny, Alex, and Celia,' " she began, pausing in hope that Grandma would notice that the letter was not addressed to her as well.

She didn't. "Go on, Henny," she encouraged.

Henny stifled another sigh. " 'Dear Henny, Alex, and Celia,' " she repeated. " 'Here we are in —' "

Whhhheeeeennnn. The sharp whine of a drill cut her off.

"Ed, what are you doing?" Grandma asked, annoyance in her voice.

"This is where you want the shelf, Stella, isn't it?" he answered.

"Yes, but —"

"I need you to help me line this up. Why don't you girls take that letter into the living room to read? It'll be quieter there."

Henny flashed Grandpa a look of surprise. But he was busy fiddling with the drill bit.

"Sure," Henny said, getting up. Alex and Celia got up, too.

Grandma looked at them, then at Grandpa with a frown. But she went over, took the shelf from Grandpa, and held it against the wall.

Henny tried to catch Grandpa's eye once more,

failed, and hurried out of the kitchen before Grandma suggested postponing the shelf mounting and listening to the letter instead.

The girls sank into the sofa, Alex and Celia on either side of Henny. Henny looked down at the letter once more and began to read aloud.

" 'Dear—' "

"You can skip that part," Alex said. "We know who it's to."

" 'Henny, Alex, and Celia,' " Henny continued, ignoring her sister. " 'Chimichihuanga is a fascinating place. Aztec architecture, much of it intact. Lovely people here, too. The weather's a bit hot. Fabulous birds and insects. Last night the weirdest bug landed right outside our cottage. It had red and green lights on it and was bright enough to read by! We have already uncovered a rare ceremonial mortar at what promises to be an important temple site.

" 'In short, we are working hard and having a swell time, except for one thing: We miss you a lot.' "

"If they miss us so much, how come they wouldn't take us with them?" Alex grumbled.

" 'And we wish you were here with us. There's a little girl here who reminds us of Celia, and we think of her—and you other two—every time we see her. We took her (or, rather, she took us) to a lake the other day. We all went swimming. We hope you're having a lot of fun with Grandma and Grandpa. We know you must be very busy.

" 'This is Mom. Dad's already fallen asleep, so I'm finishing this letter. We really do miss you. But before you know it, we'll be back and we'll tell each other all about our adventures.

" 'Little "Celia," as we call her, who's been here all evening, just tried to crawl into Dad's bed. I must take her home so I can turn in, too. Nine o'clock is my limit: Your dad and I have to be up at four A.M.!

" 'Good-night, my little chickadees. We'll write again soon. Love, Mom and Dad.' "

"That's all?" Alex said in disgust.

"You know they never write long letters," said Henny. She folded the letter and put it back in the envelope.

"Humph," said Alex.

Grandma came into the room. "Well, that didn't take long, did it?"

"Not long enough," muttered Alex.

"What was that, Alex?"

"Nothing."

"So, what did your parents have to say?"

Henny looked at Alex, who gave a slight nod. Henny handed Grandma the letter.

Grandma read it quickly. "It sounds as though they're having a good trip," she said when she finished. "We're going to have a bit of a trip today, too. Over to Bendenburg to get Celia some jeans and Alex a new pair of sneakers."

"I don't need a new pair of sneakers," Alex said, looking down at her well-worn pair with a hole over each big toe.

"Alex, the pair you're wearing almost qualify as

sandals," Grandma said, laughing at her own joke.

Alex didn't laugh back.

"Well, it's time to go," Grandma said, handing the letter back to Henny. "Bendenburg's a ways from here."

Henny got up obediently, followed by her sisters, but then she surprised herself.

"Grandma, I don't need anything," she said. "So, if you don't mind, I'd like to spend the afternoon in the library. I . . . uh . . . I'm interested in reading about the . . . uh . . . local wildlife."

Henny waited for Grandma to say no, but, instead, she smiled. "I didn't know you were interested in nature, Henny."

"I am. So, if it's okay . . ."

"Yes, it's all right, as long as you promise to stay in the library and not go off exploring on your own."

"I promise."

"Fine. We'll drop you off and pick you up at five o'clock."

"Great!"

"Well, let's go," Grandma said once again.

As they headed for the door, Alex poked Henny. "You stinker," she whispered in her ear.

"Research," Henny whispered back. "For The Lightey Club."

"Stinker," Alex mouthed again.

Nobody noticed that in all that time Celia hadn't said a word.

Henny stretched and grunted happily. The afternoon had slipped by most pleasantly. She had read through two whole books on fireflies and looked through several others on insects in general.

She looked at the big clock over the librarian's desk. It was nearly five o'clock. Grandma and her sisters would arrive soon. She sighed a little, stood up, and walked toward the exit. As she passed the desk, the librarian gave her a friendly smile. She smiled back.

She stood just outside the front door, watching for the familiar blue Ford. Five minutes passed. Then ten. Fifteen. After twenty minutes had gone by, Henny began to be a bit concerned. She did say five o'clock, didn't she?

Another five minutes went by. Maybe I ought to ask the librarian if anyone left a message for me. She turned toward the door.

"Henny!" someone called.

She turned back. It was Grandpa, and he was getting out of his mail truck. His usually calm face looked agitated.

"Grandpa! Why are you driving that today? It's your day off. And where are Grandma, Alex, and Celia?"

"They're still in Bendenburg," Grandpa said. "I was out. They just reached me on the phone. I borrowed the truck so I could pick you up and head over there."

"We're going to Bendenburg? Why?"

"Well, there's a problem."

"What kind of a problem?"

"Your sister Celia. She's disappeared."

Alex was slumped on a bench in the Bendenburg police station when Henny and Grandpa arrived. She looked subdued and unhappy.

"Where's Grandma?" asked Grandpa.

"Talking with the officer," said Alex, straightening up a little. "She said you should go right in there when you got here."

Grandpa nodded and walked through the door that Alex indicated. Alex slumped back down.

Henny sat down next to her. "What happened?" she asked.

"I don't know. We left the Jolly Jeans shop and were on our way to the Sneak-er-Round. There was a store with some super mitts in the window. I stopped to look. Grandma and Celia were walking ahead of me, and Grandma must've told Celia to wait or something while she came back to get me. I wanted to go into the sports store, but Grandma wouldn't let me. We had an argument. I lost. Then we walked back to the spot she'd left Celia at — just a little ways away in front of a bakery. Only Celia wasn't there.

"First we checked the bakery. No good. Then the other stores around it. We went back to that Jolly Jeans place, too. But she wasn't anywhere we looked. How could she have disappeared like that? It doesn't make sense. And she wouldn't have gone off with a stranger, either. Mom and Dad taught us not to do that as soon as we were old enough to walk." Alex's lower lip trembled, and she punched one fist into the palm of her other hand. "Grandma's really upset. She thinks it's all her fault."

Henny didn't say anything for a moment. Then she asked, "Was Celia acting funny at all?"

"I don't know. I was so mad at Grandma—and at you for getting to go to the library alone—I didn't pay attention. But I think maybe she was quiet. Yeah. Real quiet. She's usually all excited to go shopping and stuff, but I don't remember her saying a word the whole time."

"She was quiet this evening, too. I don't think she said anything about Mom and Dad's letter, either," Henny suddenly remembered. "Maybe it upset her."

"Upset her? Why would it upset her? I mean it was a dumb letter, but Celia doesn't get upset over dumb."

"I don't know. Maybe—" But Henny didn't finish her thought because at that precise moment the station-house door opened and an officer walked in, leading a small, sad-faced little girl by the hand.

"Celia!" Henny and Alex both yelled.

Celia took one look at them and ran into their arms.

"Where were you?" demanded Alex.

"She was at the bus station," the officer said.

"The bus station?" Henny repeated, puzzled. "Why'd you go there, Celia? You couldn't have wanted to take a bus home. You know nobody's there. Where were you going to go?"

"The airport," Celia said, in a voice so tiny they could hardly hear her.

"The airport?" said Alex. Suddenly it hit her. "You were going to try to fly to Mexico. To see Mom and Dad."

Celia nodded.

"That's crazy. You can't — " Alex began.

But Henny cut her off. "Celia, what made you feel so bad you wanted to do that?"

"The other Celia," she said in the same small voice.

"The 'other Celia'? What other Celia?"

Celia didn't answer.

But Henny did. "I think I understand," she said slowly, and from her pocket she pulled their parents' letter. She unfolded it and read, " 'There's a little girl here who reminds us of Celia.' 'We took her (or, rather, she took us) to a lake the other day. We all went swimming.' 'Little "Celia," . . . who's been here all evening, just tried to crawl into Dad's bed.' That's who you mean, right?"

Celia nodded again.

"I still don't get it. Why are you so upset about this other kid?" Alex said.

"Because," Celia whispered. She stopped, unable to continue.

"Because you think Mom and Dad love her instead of you," Henny finished for her.

Celia nodded her head once more and burst into tears.

"What a dumb thing to think," Alex said as they sat in the garden. "Mom and Dad would never dump you and adopt another kid."

Celia looked at her oldest sister. "They really wouldn't, Henny?" she asked.

"Uh-uh." Henny shook her head. "No way."

Celia nodded. "Okay. I believe you."

"I *can't* believe you made it all the way to the bus station all by yourself before anyone found you. How'd you get away from Grandma and me, anyway? We looked all over the place."

"You didn't look behind the garbage cans."

"You hid behind the garbage cans?"

"Uh-huh."

"Sheesh."

There was a pause, then Celia said, "Is Grandma still mad at me?"

"I don't think so," said Henny. "I don't think she was ever mad—just very upset."

"But you better never do that again," Alex said.

"I won't." Celia shook her head. "But I'm gonna write to Mom and Dad and tell them they better dump that other Celia."

"You can't write, dummy."

"I can so. I know Mr. M and Mr. T and Ms. A and Ms. B and . . . Anyway, Henny will help me, won't you, Henny?"

"Yes. I'll help you."

There was another pause, and then Alex said, "Hey, look, we're out here alone. Let's have a meeting of The Lightey Club."

"Goody," said Celia.

"All right," Henny said slowly. "Want to hear about Franny the Young Firefly? He once tried to run away, too, just like you did. But not for the same reason."

"What reason?"

"I'll tell you."

o   o   o

The Society for the Improvement of the Beetle Image was having its weekly meeting in the garden. Millicent Ladybug, secretary of the organization, was reciting a summary of the last meeting.

"For those of you who missed it, last week our president, Oliver Stag Beetle, presented for us the use of the stag beetle throughout history in the field of medicine. Mr. Stag Beetle himself demonstrated how the stag beetle served as stitches before they were invented. . . ."

"I wish she'd shut up, already. I want to see that fire beetle," Lightey said impatiently.

"But, Lightey, she speaks so well," tiny Drusilla the Fruitfly, who'd stayed up just for the special guest, said with surprise.

"Yeah, she can keep on speaking well—somewhere else."

"Quiet, please," Oliver boomed out at Lightey and Drusilla.

"Big shot," Lightey muttered.

"And now, our president, Oliver Stag Beetle, will introduce tonight's very special guest," Millicent was finishing.

"Tonight's very special guest has come a very long distance to speak with us tonight — all the way from South America. I am pleased to present to you Fuego the Fire Beetle."

"Wow, am I excited!" Franny the Young Firefly whispered.

And then, a rather plain but confident-looking beetle flew to the leaf that served as a stage. "*Buenos noches, amigos*. I am proud to be here tonight. I was fortunate enough to have been a stowaway on a ship that arrived in New York Harbor. The fireflies of Central Park informed me of your excellent society, so here I am."

"Hooray," Lightey cheered loudly. "Come on, all of you," he said to his fellow lightning bugs. "Here's our Society for the Improvement of the *Firefly* Image, so keep cheering."

"My name, as you have been told, is Fuego, but many call me Ford. In a few minutes I will show you why."

"Hooray," the fireflies all yelled again.

"Please," Oliver began. "I realize you're all enthusiastic — "

"Can it, Oliver," some of the rowdier fireflies howled.

Hoping to avoid trouble, Oliver shut up.

"We fire beetles come from the forests of the tropics, and we are many in number and species. One type glows green at rest and brilliant orange in flight. It is said that as Columbus was sailing along the coast of Cuba, he mistook these fire beetles for a group of native Americans carrying torches. He named the spot Cienfuegos, which means 'one hundred fires.' Another type, like a caterpillar in appearance, has a red headlight and green sidelights. It is nicknamed the Railroad Worm. The light of many a single fire beetle, including my breed, is equal proportionally to the glow of the brightest star. A human could read a book by it."

"Hooray," the fireflies shouted, and all lit up at once.

"*Sí, mis amigos*. Still, none of these can beat you American fireflies," he added graciously.

"Hooray!"

"Now, I shall show you why my nickname is Ford." And the fire beetle turned on his lights — two white ones in front and a red one at the rear, just like an automobile's head and taillights.

"Ooooh," gasped everyone.

"Bravo! Bravo!" shouted Lightey, and he and the other lightning bugs rushed at Fuego and flew him around the garden.

"Hmmm, Ed and Stella must be having a party," said a neighbor, peering out her window at the lights. "And they didn't invite us. Well, I won't do them any favors in a hurry."

"Order! Order! Stop! Stop!" bellowed Oliver as the fireflies whipped Fuego around the yard.

"Ruffians! They're not fit to be included in the beetle race," Millicent huffed, horrified.

Some of the beetles agreed with her, but others got even more excited and began to do a fast crawl around the garden; a few tried somersaults and ended up on their backs with their legs kicking in the air. Several unwelcome cockroaches, hearing the hubbub, came out of their hiding places and began to raid the refreshments Millicent had so carefully gathered and arranged especially for this occasion. Fortunately, the roaches were thrown out by a group of solemn sexton beetles. The other beetles continued their party, unaware (except for Oliver and Millicent) that Lightey and his crew had flown off with Fuego to their section of the garden.

"I've never met a celebrity before," Drusilla said, bug-eyed.

"*Muchas gracias*, my child, but I am no celebrity," Fuego said.

"To us you are," Franny said. "You're different and exciting. We hardly ever get to meet anyone so . . . so . . . colorful."

"Let's not overdo it, Franny," Lightey warned rather harshly. The truth is that he felt hurt because Franny, whom he had taken under his very own wing, was paying a lot of attention to Fuego. But he added hastily, "You'll embarrass our guest."

"Do not worry. I am not easily embarrassed," Fuego said easily.

"Tell us about your adventures, *Señor* Fuego," said

Jerome, Lightey's best friend, who was proud of his knowledge of Spanish.

"Yes, tell us," the others cried.

"There is not so much to tell," Fuego said.

"You're just being modest," Jerome said. "Here our biggest worry is avoiding a few birds, but you must have to defend yourself against birds and lizards and snakes and all kinds of things. The creatures you must see! Here the only people we know are the Geffens and a few of their neighbors. You must see native Americans, explorers, and adventurers! Here we—"

"Quit it, already, will ya," snapped Lightey. "And let Ford tell us himself."

So Fuego began to tell of his adventures in the jungle—how he nearly got eaten by a lizard; how, on a dare, he spent a night in a cotinga's nest; how he nearly drowned once during the rainy season and was actually rescued by a native girl who took him home and released him after the rains had ended.

The fireflies and other insects who had joined the crowd were spellbound. Lightey was, too; but, at the same time, he felt something else: jealousy.

"I think we should let our guest rest now," Lightey said during a break in Fuego's story.

"Yes, I think I should like that. I have a long journey ahead tomorrow night."

"Must you leave tomorrow?" Franny protested, and the others joined in.

"Yes, Bright One, I must."

So Fuego went off to sleep, and the bugs slowly went to their places, talking all the way about Fuego's fantastic adventures.

"He is the most amazing bug I've ever met," Franny said to Lightey.

"You're overdoing it again," Lightey answered.

"He called me Bright One."

"Oh, brother. Next you'll ask for his antenna print or a bit of his glow powder to remember him by."

"Stop it, Lightey. You don't know a real hero when you see one. A hero who's traveled the world."

The remark stung Lightey. "My grandmother led a troop of fireflies out of captivity. My grandfather donated himself to science. My parents were real leaders of their community. As for me, I not only rescued our community from the Blue Jay, but I . . . I . . . spent a week in . . . Japan! And you tell me I don't know a hero!"

"Okay, Lightey, I didn't mean it, so stop losing your temper."

But Lightey, still hurt, flew off without saying another word.

Alone, Franny stayed up the whole morning and thought and thought. Lightey's been to Japan, and Fuego's a world traveler, but where have I been? When afternoon came, he had made up his mind: He would go to South America with Fuego and learn the secrets of the fire beetles. He was so excited by his decision that, on the spot, he rushed off to where the visitor was resting.

"Mr. Fuego," he said as quietly as he could.

"Hmmm. Ah, the Bright One. Is it time for me to leave already?"

"No, Mr. Fuego. I just wanted to tell you that I'm going with you."

"Oh, that is nice," said the sleepy Fuego, who hadn't the faintest idea of what Franny was saying.

"Gee, that's great. See you this evening, Mr. Fuego. And thanks."

On his way back to his leaf, Franny passed Lightey, whose injured pride had kept him from sleeping well.

"What are you doing?" Lightey demanded wearily.

"Oh, nothing."

"You were visiting Fuego, weren't you?"

"No, well, yes. I wanted to see if he needed anything."

"You're a silly bug. Go to bed."

Franny spent the rest of the day getting ready to go. Not that he had much to do. He kept checking to see whether Fuego was up yet and dreaming about life in South America. He didn't dare tell his friends he was leaving: He knew they'd laugh or try to stop him or flash the news to his mother—or all three.

That evening, he hid under a daisy and watched all the bugs line up to say good-bye to the fire beetle.

"I'm surprised Franny's not here. He seemed so thrilled by Señor Fuego's stories," Jerome said.

"Yeah, I'm surprised, too," Lightey replied, beginning to worry a bit. "Let's go talk to him after Ford leaves."

But while they looked for Franny, he was already flying swiftly after the departed Fuego.

"Here I am," he said proudly, when he caught up with the fire beetle.

"Well, Bright One, have you come to say good-bye?"

"Good-bye? No, don't you remember? I'm going with you."

"With me? Oh, no. That would never work." Fuego began to laugh.

"Why not? You said it would be nice."

"*Mi amigo*, you are a New York firefly, not a South American fire beetle. The jungle is not for you."

"I'm tired of the Geffens' yard. I want adventure. I want to learn the secrets of the fire beetles." He stopped suddenly, afraid he'd gone too far.

But the fire beetle already had an idea. "All right, Bright One, you can come with me. I can promise you plenty of adventures."

After a very, very, very long flight, they arrived at a dock and flew to the deck of a ship anchored there. Franny was glad to rest; he'd never been so faraway from home before. But before long, the ship was lurching and swaying and shoving off.

Meanwhile, Lightey and Jerome naturally hadn't found Franny, and both began to get really worried. "This isn't like him," Jerome said.

"You said it," Lightey answered.

They flew around the garden, asking every bug they saw about Franny. Finally, one firefly said, "I thought I saw him hot-winging it in Fuego's direction."

"Oh, no, that's just what I was afraid of," Lightey groaned.

"What should we do?" Jerome cried.

"Down to the docks. We'll see if the ship has sailed." And off they raced.

Back at the ship, which had only been at sea for a short time, Franny was feeling a little less adventuresome and a little more seasick.

"How long will it take?"

"Quite awhile," Fuego answered, and Franny was silent. The sky was very dark; there were no leaves, no flowers, no fireflies, and no friends, except for the brave fire beetle.

"We had better find our quarters," Fuego said, and led the increasingly homesick Franny to the ship's hold. They glowed faintly to see the way. Suddenly, Franny's light caught something's bright red eyes.

"Help!" he yelled. "What is that?"

"A rat," Fuego answered quietly. "Go quickly back on deck."

But that was enough for Franny. "Home! I want to go home!" he squeaked.

"But we are out at sea."

"Home! Home! Home!" was all he could say.

Fuego had been quite certain that this was just what would happen, and he knew just what to do,

but he pretended not to. "You wanted adventure. You should have thought of the dangers before you left."

"Home! Home! Home!" Franny insisted.

"I don't know, *mi amigo.* . . ." Fuego paused for a long time. Then he said, "Wait, I have an idea." And he began to flash his bright lights.

Jerome and Lightey had just reached the dock when they saw something that looked like a beacon. "Ford/Fuego!" they yelled together, and flew toward the lights.

"Please be careful," Franny said to Fuego. "The sailors might see you and catch us."

"What is that light?" a sailor said as Fuego and Franny slipped under a board.

The sailor searched and then scratched his head. "I must be seeing things."

"You stay put," Fuego said to Franny. After that, Fuego would flash and then dive to another hiding place each time a sailor yelled, "What is that light?"

Jerome and Lightey followed the flashes until they reached the ship and quietly slipped on board.

"Here," Fuego whispered.

"Where is he?" Lightey asked. "Franny, you fool, come out."

"Lightey!" Franny yelled, and leaped from his hiding place. "And Jerome."

"Don't Lightey me, you idiot," Lightey said gruffly, fighting back his urge to cry. "Say good-bye to Ford, and let's go." Then, as casually as he could, Lightey turned to Fuego. "Oh, and thanks a lot."

"Do not mention it," Fuego said.

"Have a safe journey," Jerome added.

"I will be quite fine, thank you. Good-bye, Bright One."

"That was dumb, dumb, dumb. You'd have worried your mother to death." Lightey bawled out poor Franny all the way home. "Dumb, dumb, dumb."

Franny was so glad to be going home that he let Lightey yell.

When they reached the Geffens' garden, the other fireflies were waiting. "Hooray, Franny! The world traveler!" they teased. "Hooray!"

"Dumb, dumb, dumb," Lightey muttered.

"Okay, that's enough. You're right," Franny said. Then he turned to Lightey. "But I bet you never have been to Japan."

"Humph," said Lightey. Franny was right.

o   o   o

Henny finished the story and looked at Celia to see how she'd liked it. Celia's chin was resting on her chest. Her head snapped up. "Did Franny have a good time in South America?" she asked, too loudly.

"He never got to South America, dopey," Alex said, not unkindly. "He got scared and Lightey brought him back home."

"He did? I didn't hear that part."

"Of course you didn't. You slept through the end of the story."

"I did? Oh, Henny could you tell it again?"

"Okay," Henny said. "Well, Franny and Fuego got to the ship, and Lightey and Jerome decided to —"

Celia let out a loud snore.

Henny stopped speaking and laughed.

"And they all lived happily ever after," Alex finished.

Henny laughed again and shook her head. "Poor Celia. You think she'll be okay now?"

"She better be. I don't want to go through that hassle again."

Henny nodded and thought that this time it was Alex who'd sounded just like their dad.

Chapter 7

Celia recovered quickly from her runaway attempt, but it looked as if Grandma hadn't. When Celia went outside to take in the newspaper, Grandma followed her. When Henny asked to go to the library alone again, Grandma said no. And when Jimmy Cox called to invite Alex to come to a big game on Saturday, Grandma turned down the invitation without even asking Alex if she wanted to go. Alex found out about it and got so angry that she threatened to run away just like Celia had.

Henny was there for the argument, and when Alex yelled, "Only when *I* run away, you'll never find me," she saw Grandma's face do a peculiar thing. The only way she could describe it was to say that it slipped. In place of Grandma's strong, determined face, there was a sad, scared one Henny had never seen before. It was present only for a moment, but Henny wondered if it had been there other times and she just hadn't seen it.

Grandma turned to look at the seat Celia usually occupied at the kitchen table and noticed that she wasn't there. "Where is Celia?" she asked, an edge of panic in her voice.

"In the bathroom," Henny told her.

Grandma inhaled deeply and turned back to Alex. "Perhaps you can go to another game," she said, trying to keep her voice calm. "But this Saturday we have company coming."

"Who is it, Grandma?" Henny asked, trying to lighten the mood.

Grandma's face changed again. It got softer, and her eyes went all shiny. "It's a surprise," she said. She smiled, and Henny could tell she was really pleased about whoever it was.

Henny hoped she would be, too.

"Who do you think it is?" Henny asked that night.

"Probably some dumb member of the Do-Our-Part Club," Alex muttered. She was still angry, but not as angry as she'd been before. The truth was she felt a little bad about threatening to run away because she knew how upset Grandma—and everyone else, herself included—had gotten over Celia.

"I don't think so," said Henny, remembering Grandma's look.

"I know who it is," Celia said, bouncing on her bed. "It's Mom and Dad!"

"It's not Mom and Dad, dummy," Alex said. "They won't be back for two more weeks."

Henny frowned at Alex and then looked at Celia to make sure she wasn't upset. She needn't have worried. Celia bounced down on her backside and then back up to her feet and said, "Who do you think it is, Henny?"

"I don't know. Uncle Mark and Aunt Bryna?"

At their names, Alex perked up. Uncle Mark and Aunt Bryna were both gym teachers. Uncle Mark's favorite sport was hockey; Aunt Bryna's was basketball. But they both liked baseball, too. They might even want to go to the game Jimmy's team was playing. "Uncle Mark and Aunt Bryna! All right!" Alex pumped a fist in the air.

"Hey, wait a minute," Henny said. "It might not be them."

"Well, then who else could it be?" Alex asked, hands on her hips.

Henny thought a minute and shrugged. "We'll find out on Saturday," she said.

Saturday finally arrived, and the three sisters were excited. All week they'd tried to guess who the surprise guest was going to be. And they'd tried the guesses out on Grandma. It was Alex who started it.

"Hey, Grandma. Is it Uncle Mark and Aunt Bryna?" she'd asked.

"I'm not going to tell you," Grandma'd answered.

"How about Cousin Shelley?" Henny tried. She

thought she saw Grandma's eyes flicker for an instant.

But Grandma only tapped her pursed lips and mumbled, "My lips are sealed."

"Well, I sure hope it's not Mason Fiedler," Alex grumbled.

Henny and Celia began to giggle.

"Who on earth is Mason Fiedler, and what's wrong with him?" asked Grandma.

"He's Mom and Dad's boss. He smokes big cigars and has bad breath."

"No, it's not Mason Fiedler," said Grandma. "At least, I *hope* not."

Henny and Celia'd giggled harder. Alex joined in, and, to their pleasant surprise, so did Grandma.

Now Grandma and the three girls were waiting in the living room for Grandpa to return with their guest (or guests).

"I still think it's Uncle Mark and Aunt Bryna," Alex whispered to Henny.

"I don't think so," said Henny, even though Uncle Mark and Aunt Bryna had been her guess first. "They have —"

She was interrupted by the sound of Grandpa's car pulling up.

"They're here," said Grandma. She went to the door, and the girls all followed her.

Henny found herself taking a big breath as Grandma pulled the door open.

Grandpa was walking up the path to the door. At his side was a boy a year or two older than Henny. He had fair hair, blue eyes, and a healthy tan.

Around his neck was a pair of binoculars. In one hand he carried a small suitcase and in the other a rather large net. Henny didn't recognize him at all.

"You know they did this study of spider webs. Really interesting. They gave the spiders LSD—" The boy stopped speaking when he heard Grandma say "You're here." Then he was up the steps in one bound. He leaned the net against the door jamb, reached for Grandma's hand, and shook it vigorously. "Hello," he said in a big voice. "It's good to meet you finally, Grandma."

"Grandma?" Alex's voice cracked.

"Who is it? I can't see," Celia piped up, trying to push between her sisters.

"Girls," Grandma said, "let me introduce you to your cousin, Ellis Foster, Aunt Jocelyn's son."

Henny blinked. Aunt Jocelyn. She was Mom and Uncle Mark's sister, which also made her Grandma's daughter. But Grandma didn't talk about her—or to her, for that matter. They'd had a big argument a long time ago. Henny vaguely remembered her parents' discussing it. It was over Aunt Jocelyn's husband, Uncle Bret. Grandma hadn't wanted them to marry in the first place. And then Uncle Bret had done something wrong. Henny could almost remember what it was, but not quite. She was certain her parents had mentioned it and she'd forgotten. She was also certain they *hadn't* mentioned Cousin Ellis.

And now there he was, standing right in front of them.

Henny turned to look at Grandma and noticed that her face was flushed and her eyes all shiny again.

"Ellis," Grandma continued, "these are your cousins Henny, Alex, and Celia."

"You're our cousin?" said Celia.

"Yes," Ellis answered.

"Then how come we never heard of you?" asked Alex.

Ellis looked at Grandma for an explanation.

She didn't give any. Instead, she patted Celia's curly head and said, "Lunch is ready. Are you hungry, Ellis?"

Ellis, realizing that Grandma wasn't going to answer Alex's question, smiled and said, "Hungry as a praying mantis in July."

Henny did a double take. "Praying mantis?" she said involuntarily.

"Yes. Did you know in South America there are praying mantises that eat birds, lizards, and frogs? Praying mantises are always hungry."

"That's interesting information," Grandma said, with genuine admiration in her voice. "You certainly know a lot about praying mantises."

"He knows a lot about all kinds of insects," Grandpa put in. "He wants to be a . . . what did you call it?"

"An entomologist."

"Right. Someone who studies bugs. Well, you'll find plenty of bugs around here," Grandpa said.

"I know. I saw a *Vanessa atalanta* and a *Nymphalis antiopa* as we drove from the station."

"Henny knows a lot about bugs, too," Celia piped up loyally.

Henny said nothing. For some reason she didn't quite understand, her stomach had begun to hurt.

"You do?" Ellis said, with a big smile. "Did you know that after two mantises mate, the female eats the male?"

"Ellis, somehow I don't think this conversation goes well with lunch," Grandma said.

"I guess you're right," Ellis said, still smiling.

Henny didn't feel like smiling back.

But all through lunch, Ellis continued to pepper the conversation with tidbits about bugs. He told them about complex experiments done on cockroaches to develop better roach traps. He discussed the difficulties in identifying and classifying certain beetles. He described in great detail what happens in a beehive when the queen dies or is removed by scientists studying the hive.

The more he talked, the more Henny's stomach hurt. She still wasn't sure why. After all, she liked learning things. And Ellis sure knew a lot — especially about science. He began three-quarters of his sentences with the words "Scientists say."

"Does your mommy like bugs, too?" asked Celia when they'd gotten to dessert.

"Not really," Ellis said with a smile.

"How about your daddy?"

Ellis stopped smiling. "My father doesn't live with us."

"Where does he live?"

"Celia," Grandma cut in. "Your ice cream is melting."

"He lives in . . . Arizona," Ellis answered.

"Oh," said Celia, and she scooped up the rest of her chocolate chip.

Arizona. Something buzzed in Henny's head, but before she could grab it, it was gone.

"Well, now, Grandpa and I can take care of these dishes. Before we go on a tour of our town, why don't you children go out into the garden? There are plenty of fascinating insects there."

"No!" Henny said loudly.

Everyone looked at her. She turned beet red.

"Is something wrong, Henny?" Grandma asked.

Yes, something's wrong. Don't make us take Ellis into the garden. Please don't. "I . . . just thought it might . . . it might rain," she said feebly.

Grandma gave her a funny look. "Nonsense. The sun's shining away. Go on out now, all of you."

Feeling miserable, Henny got up and led Ellis and her sisters outside.

A small, white butterfly fluttered past them. "*Pieris rapae*," Ellis identified it. A beetle skittered across the porch steps. "*Calosoma frigidum*. Boy, this is a great garden. How far back does it go?"

"Far," said Celia.

"Not that far," said Henny at the same time.

"Here, let's sit down on these steps."

"No, I want to walk along this path," Ellis said.

Henny, Alex, and Celia had no choice but to follow him until he came to the bench and chairs.

"Neat!" he said, plunking himself down. Another butterfly flew by. "Hey, that's a white admiral! I'm going to bring my net and jar out here later."

"Your net and jar? What do you need a net and jar for?" asked Alex.

"To catch some butterflies. I collect them."

"How many do you have?"

"Over fifty."

"Where do you keep them?" asked Celia.

"In my room."

"Does your mommy mind them?"

"Not the butterflies. She doesn't like the beetles very much."

"You have pet beetles?"

Suddenly Henny said, "Why don't we go in now? Grandma and Grandpa must be ready to take us on our tour."

But her voice was too low, and Ellis didn't move. "They're not pets," he explained patiently to Celia and Alex. "They're for study. I keep them in three cases."

"Don't they get bored in there?" asked Celia.

"No. Butterflies and beetles aren't like people. They don't get bored. And even if they did, these wouldn't."

"Why not?"

"Because they aren't alive."

"You mean you've got a bunch of dead bugs in your room?" Alex said. "How'd you find so many dead ones?"

Henny's head began to ache along with her stomach. "I said, let's go in . . ." She tried to speak louder but her voice came out squeaky. Thoughts and words swirled around in her brain. Cousin Ellis. Aunt Jocelyn. Uncle Bret who . . .

"They weren't dead when I found them. I caught them with my net and put them in the killing jar."

"You mean you killed them?" Alex said, shocked.

"Yes."

"You killed them?" Celia repeated. "You killed the bugs?"

"You have to kill them to study them. That's what entomologists do. Don't worry. The bugs don't feel anything. I use carbon tetrachloride. I'll show you later."

"Oh, no, you won't," Alex said. "You won't kill any bugs in this garden."

"Don't let him hurt Lightey!" Celia wailed.

"I won't," said Alex.

"Lightey? Who's Lightey?"

Celia was so upset that she forgot about her promise of secrecy. "He's a lightning bug," she whimpered.

"Oh. Don't worry. I've already got a lightning bug." He tried to pat Celia, but she pulled away. "Anyway, they won't be around much longer, so we should enjoy them while we can."

"What do you mean, they won't be around much longer?" asked Alex.

"They only live three or four weeks. They mate, lay eggs, and then, by early or maybe mid-August, they all die."

"No!" said Alex.

"Lightey!" cried Celia.

It was then that something in Henny's brain snapped. "Your father . . . your father—he's in Arizona, all right. He's in the Arizona State Prison. Your father's a crook."

Chapter 8

It was twilight. Grandpa, Alex, and Celia were
watching TV. Grandma was in bed with a headache, and Henny was in the garden alone,
watching the fireflies twinkling green-gold in and
out of the leaves and against the darkening sky.
There weren't as many of them as there had been a
few weeks ago. Ellis was right: By August they'd all
be gone. It was something she'd read but hadn't
wanted to think about.

She thought of Ellis again and heaved a big sigh.
The name pricked her conscience like a wasp's sting.
How could I have been so awful. How could I have
said such a terrible thing, Henny thought. It was
true, but that doesn't make it any better. In fact, it
makes it worse. At least he knew his father is in

prison and just didn't want us to know. If he hadn't known . . . Henny shuddered at the thought of how bad it would've been if Ellis had found out about his dad from Henny in that mean way. Nobody deserved to be hurt like that—not even a bug murderer.

Henny looked out at the fireflies again. Science or no science, it didn't seem right, snuffing out an insect's life so you could put it in a case just to study it. It didn't seem right that fireflies would live such a short time, either. She shuddered once more. Gloom was settling on her shoulders as heavy as a sack of soil. She faintly heard the back door open, then someone crunch on the gravel path toward her.

In another moment, Grandpa loomed before her. "It's a nice night," he said. "Mind if I join you?"

"Okay," Henny said in a low voice. She didn't really want any company, but she couldn't say "Go away."

After a few moments of silence, Grandpa said, "Well, Ellis's bus must be miles from here by now."

Henny didn't reply.

"You missed a good tour. We went up to the old mill. I haven't been there in months. Saw a lot of interesting bugs—"

"Grandpa, let's not talk about bugs," Henny cut in.

"All right. How's your tummy?"

"Not so good."

"I'll fix you some peppermint tea—with fresh mint. Grew it myself. Always good for the tummy."

"Then you do take care of this garden."

"Sure. Didn't you know that?"

"No. We were wondering if you did, Celia, Alex, and I. We never saw you work in it."

"Well, you haven't been around much on Saturdays. Plus I do a lot of weeding in the early morning before you get up."

There was another period of silence. Then Henny said, "What I did to Ellis was awful, wasn't it?"

"Not so bad," Grandpa said. "We all make mistakes. Even you."

"Grandma thinks it was bad. This was supposed to be a special occasion, wasn't it? All of us meeting Ellis. I ruined it. Grandma told me she was 'terribly disappointed' in me."

"She'll get over it. That's just your grandmother's way. She expects a lot from everyone. Maybe too much. And the one she expects the most from is herself. Nobody else is as hard on Stella as she is."

Henny took in Grandpa's words and thought about them. Then she said, "Is Grandma happy?"

"Sometimes she is, sometimes she isn't, just like the rest of us. I think she's having a hard time trying to keep you all happy."

"But she doesn't have to try to keep us happy," Henny blurted out. "I mean, if she let us alone, we'd be happy."

"Maybe you should tell her that, Henny," Grandpa said.

"I can't."

"Why not? You just told me."

"I know, but you're not"—the word surprised her almost as much as this conversation had—"scary," she said in a low voice.

Grandpa had the sense not to laugh or even say a word.

It was awhile before he spoke again, and then he said, "Pretty fireflies. I've counted at least ten."

"They're dying," Henny said.

"They're what?"

"Dying. Ellis told me."

"Oh," Grandpa said, in a tone that indicated he suddenly understood something. "Well, there will be new ones next year."

"I don't want new ones. It won't be the same," Henny said, her voice breaking.

"Lightey?" Grandpa said gently.

Henny turned to him. "You *were* here!"

Grandpa didn't respond.

After a pause, Henny said, "We have a club, Alex, Celia, and I. I tell stories about Lightey and his friends."

"Sounds neat. . . . I don't suppose you could use another member?"

Henny stared at Grandpa, but in the darkness she couldn't make out his expression. "You want to join?"

"Sure. If you'll have me."

"I have to ask Alex and Celia."

"Want me to get them for you?"

"Yes. And then could you wait for us inside until we call you?"

"Okay."

Grandpa got up and went into the house. In a few moments, Alex and Celia came out.

"You feeling better, Henny?" Celia asked.

"I think so."

"Boy, you sure let Ellis have it."

"No, I didn't, Alex. It was bad what I did. I was nasty. I should have told him I didn't want to hear about science, science, science."

Alex thought over what Henny said. "Yeah, I guess you're right. Anyway, I'm glad you shut him up."

"Are we having a Lightey Club meeting?" Celia asked, ignoring the whole question of Ellis and how to treat him.

"Well, as a matter of fact, that's what I wanted to talk to you about. See, Grandpa found out about our club."

"He did?" said Celia.

"How?" demanded Alex.

"I told him," Henny answered simply.

"Hey, The Lightey Club was supposed to be a secret," Alex said angrily.

"I know. It still is, but now Grandpa's in on it. Anyway, he wants to be a member."

"He does?" Celia put in.

"Yes. So we have to vote on it. That's how clubs work. How many in favor of Grandpa's becoming a member of The Lightey Club?"

"Me," said Celia.

Alex was silent.

"How many against?"

"I'm against," said Alex. "He'll tell Grandma."

"I don't think he will."

"Why not?"

"Because . . . because he didn't tell her he found me in the garden that morning."

Alex thought for a long time. Finally she said, "Okay. We'll give him a chance. When should we have our first meeting together?"

"Now!" said Celia.

"Not now," said Alex. "It's already almost past your bedtime."

"I'll go right to bed after. Please."

"Okay, okay," said Alex. "You don't have to yell. Go and get Grandpa."

"All right!" said Celia, imitating Alex.

"Oh, brother," said Alex.

Quicker than a worm wiggles, Celia was back with Grandpa in tow.

"This Lightey Club meeting is ordered," she said.

Alex snorted. "Is *called to order*, dummy."

"Is called to order," Celia repeated. "Okay, Henny. You can tell the story now."

Henny cleared her throat and began:

o o o

It was a hot and lazy summer evening, and neither Lightey nor Jerome had the energy to glow, let alone fly around.

"I'm getting bored. I want to do something good for bugdom," Lightey the Lightning Bug said.

"Yeah? What do you want to do?" asked his good friend Jerome.

"I don't know, but something's got to happen or I'll make it happen."

"It's too hot to do anything, good for bugdom or not," Jerome said.

But Lightey wasn't listening. He was busy thinking.

The two bugs sat in silence for a while.

"That's it," Lightey suddenly shouted.

"Arghhh," choked Jerome, losing his balance and frantically beating his wings to steady himself.

Lightey didn't notice Jerome's upset and continued, "We will donate ourselves to science."

Jerome managed to regain his perch. "Uh, would you mind repeating that? I'm sure I couldn't have heard you right."

"I said we will donate ourselves to science."

"I heard you right, all right. You're nuts—absolutely, positively nuts. You want to die so you can do something good? And you have the nerve to want me to go with you?" Jerome yelled.

In a calm voice, Lightey said, "Did I say anything about dying? No. I happen to know that scientists want to study our lights. All they do is examine us, take a bit of our glow powder, do a few experiments, and let us go."

"Yeah, and how do you happen to know all this?"

"Because my grandfather did it, and he told my mother, who told me. That's how," Lightey said triumphantly.

Jerome said nothing. Then he sighed. "Where would we have to go?"

"To the lab," said Lightey.

"Where's that?"

Lightey told him.

When he finished, Franny popped out from under a leaf. "I'm coming, too," he said. "I want to do something . . . noble. And you're not going to stop me. You and Jerome are going, so there's no reason I can't."

Lightey sighed. He was too hot to fight. "All right, Franny, I won't try to stop you. We'll meet here tomorrow morning."

The next day was hotter than the one before. Lightey was sound asleep when Jerome and Franny awakened him.

"Okay, get up!" they yelled.

"Blaaaa!" Lightey jumped.

"Time to be noble," Jerome said.

"What? What day is this? Where am I?"

"Tuesday, same place as usual, and we're going to help bugdom."

"Huh?"

"We're going to donate ourselves to science, remember?"

"Oh, yeah. Just let me pull myself together." Then Lightey noticed Twinky was with them. "What are you doing here?" he asked.

"I'm going to join you."

"You can't join us. You're a butterfly, not a firefly," Franny said.

"I know I'm a butterfly, but where you're going is the same place they tag monarchs. My friend Alexandria told me."

"What are you talking about?"

"Scientists tag monarchs to see how far they migrate. When I migrate, I'll let someone remove my tag and send it back here. Get it?"

"No," said Jerome and Franny.

"Yeah, sure," said Lightey, who didn't want to seem ignorant. "But are you sure that's where they do it?"

"I'm sure."

"All right, then, you can come with us."

"Hello, bugs. What are you all doing?" another voice said.

Whirling and fluttering around, they saw Gloria the Garden Spider.

"Having a chat," Jerome answered.

"Oh."

"We're kind of busy, Gloria," Lightey said.

"That's all right. Don't pay any attention to me — I'm just a garden spider, anyway."

"Come on, Gloria."

"It's true. Nothing ever happens to me. Life is so unexciting. Here I am, an artist, but no one appreciates me. I'm thinking of donating myself to science."

"That's what we're doing. Oops," said Twinky.

"Twinky!" yelled Lightey, Jerome, and Franny.

"You are? Right now? I'll go with you."

"Oh, no, Gloria. You see, we'll all be released, but how do we know what they'd do to you?"

"I already know — I heard about it from an orb spider. They just let me spin and then they study my web. Then they release me. At least scientists appreciate art."

"Jeez, this is turning into a parade. All right, you can come with us," Lightey said. "But nobody else."

So the group set off for the laboratory. It wasn't very far, but it took a long time because Gloria couldn't fly, and the bugs finally took turns carrying her, which slowed them down considerably. Eventually, they arrived and entered the cool, white building. Up the stairs they went. Into a room they flew and settled on a gleaming white table.

"How did these get here?" a scientist said when he entered the room.

"Beats me," said another.

"Well, we might as well use them."

"Take the butterfly and the spider to the respective labs. I'll handle the fireflies."

"Meet you at the exit," Twinky whispered to the bugs.

"Ditto," said Gloria.

"Now, you mustn't be scared, Franny," Lightey said, his voice shaking slightly.

"I'm not," said Franny.

"I am," said Jerome.

And they were whisked away to another room, where scientists carefully examined and prodded and took samples and conducted experiments. Then they were released.

"That was dumb," Jerome said when they met

outside. "Flashing a flashlight as a signal. Did they think we'd fall for that and think it was another firefly? Dumb."

"It had a scientific purpose," Lightey said, thinking to himself that Jerome was right. "I hope you played along."

"Of course, but it was still dumb."

"I thought it was fun, especially when they used different colored lights," Franny said. "And, besides, now I've done something for bugdom."

All at once, a frightened Twinky rushed up to them, a paper tag on her wing. "Oh, my goodness, I'm glad I found you. Something awful is going to happen to Gloria."

"What!" the three yelled in unison.

"I sneaked back in after they released me, and I flew from door to door to find her—to see how she was doing. I heard them say they'd give her the drug tomorrow."

"Drug? What drug?" Lightey asked.

"I don't know, but I followed a scientist into another room. And . . . Oh, it's too horrible to describe."

"Go on, Twink."

"Well, I saw three spiders in glass cases spinning these crooked, awful webs. And I heard a scientist say, 'After we've tested a few more, we can write up a positive statement about its effects.' I know he was talking about the drug—and about Gloria, who's next. Oh, Lightey, we must save her."

"Let me think, Twink. It's getting dark. We can

probably sneak in unnoticed. Franny, you stand guard." The truth was he didn't want to endanger the young firefly. "Twink, lead us and then make yourself scarce — you stand out too much."

Through a crack above a window, the three slipped in. Twinky led them to Gloria's room.

"The door's closed tight," Jerome said. "What'll we do?"

"Wait," was all Lightey could say. "Twink, you'd better go."

"I'll wait outside," she said anxiously. "Good luck."

For a long time, they waited. Just as they were losing hope, the door swung open. A scientist looked out.

"You can clean up now," she said to a passing attendant.

"I've got to finish the moth room first," he answered.

"Okay, see you tomorrow," she said, leaving. And as she did, Lightey and Jerome slipped in.

"Gloria, Gloria," they called.

"Lightey, Jerome, is that you?"

"Yes. Where are you?"

"Here."

"Where?"

"In this box."

And there was Gloria in a wooden cage dotted with a few tiny air holes.

"Gloria, we've got to get you out."

"Why? I'm going to *create* tomorrow."

"Gloria, listen. Twinky overheard them. They're going to give you a drug that makes your webs go funny."

"I don't believe you."

"Gloria, it's true."

"Yeah, it's true—they do it all the time," said a funny voice.

"Who's that?" asked Lightey.

"Me. Fred the Roach, fleet of feet and nimble of brain," said an ugly cockroach, stepping out of his crack in the wall.

"You frightened us," Jerome said.

"Well, I'm the strong, silent type," he replied.

"You say they'll really drug me?" Gloria asked, pained.

"Yep. Always do."

"Doesn't anyone appreciate natural talent?" Gloria cried.

"Forget about that now. We've got to get you out of here, and fast," said Lightey, thinking about the attendant and their last chance to leave before morning.

"If you don't mind my saying so, I think I can help you bugs," Fred said.

"How?" Lightey and Jerome asked, while Gloria sat crying in her cage.

"I can chew through the wood."

"How fast?"

"Not fast enough—by myself. But I happen to have a few friends. Bugsy, Fats, Matilda, come and get it," he yelled.

Out zipped three equally ugly roaches (especially Fats). They got to work, nibbling a small hole in the box — on the underside so it wouldn't be seen by the scientists. They were still chewing when the door opened and the attendant entered.

"Oh, no, he's here already," Jerome said.

"Just be quiet and, for goodness sake, Gloria, stop that crying." And while the attendant arranged the room, the roaches finished.

"Okay," Fred said. "Job done. See you around again sometime."

"Thanks a lot," Lightey said.

"Don't mention it," said Fred, and crawled back into the wall with his three friends.

Quietly, Gloria crawled out of the hole and, accompanied by Lightey and Jerome, down to the door. When the attendant opened it, they slipped out and raced to the exit, as fast as they could with Gloria on their backs.

"Gloria!" Twinky and Franny yelled when they saw her. "Lightey, Jerome, you did it!"

"No one appreciates art," the stunned Gloria was still muttering.

"Yeah. Looks like we did a couple of services for bugdom," Lightey said proudly. "Even though Gloria's not really a bug."

"Helped out by four roaches," Jerome added.

"Roaches?" Twinky said.

"Yeah, well, they helped a little . . . but we did most of the work."

"Lightey," warned Jerome.

"Okay—it was a fifty-fifty job. But we better not let this get out or we'll be plagued by a bunch of conceited roaches. There's nothing worse than a swell-headed roach."

"Except for a swell-headed lightning bug," Jerome teased.

"Except for a swell-headed lightning . . . huh?" said Lightey, when he realized what he was saying.

"Except for a swell-headed lightning bug," said Jerome, Twinky, and Franny in chorus. And they laughed.

o   o   o

After the story, Alex and Celia went inside, but Grandpa stayed outside with Henny. "Thanks for letting me join your club," he said.

"I'm glad you did," Henny said.

"You coming in now? Or you want a few minutes alone?"

"A few minutes alone, please."

"Okay." Grandpa started walking up the path. As he did, he said, "I wonder if Lightey knows he's immortal now." He was gone before Henny had a chance to ask him what he meant.

Henny leaned against the bench and closed her eyes. In another moment, Lightey was by her side.

"You're going away, aren't you?" Henny said.

"Yes—and no."

"What do you mean?"

"You won't see me, but I'll still be there."

"What do you mean?" Henny repeated.

"Don't you see, Henny? You've made me live forever."

"Me? How?"

"In your stories, of course," he said, with a touch of impatience.

"Really?"

"Boy, you humans aren't as clever as I thought you were."

"No, we're not," said Henny.

There was a pause. Then Lightey said, "So, thanks."

"Don't mention it."

"Don't worry—I won't," Lightey said with a smile. "See you around." And he took off into the air.

Henny's eyes blinked open. It was still pitch-dark in the garden, and this time there was no sign of Grandpa. She stood up and felt lighter. "I'll write Ellis a letter," she said aloud. Then she went into the house.

Chapter 9

Henny was proud of her letter to Ellis. It had taken her three days to write. In it, she not only apologized, but she also told him why she'd gotten so upset. She hoped he'd understand, but even if he didn't at least she'd put her feelings down on paper.

She went to Grandma and asked for Ellis's address so she could mail the letter. Grandma was impressed. "That shows a lot of maturity, Henny," she said. "We can drop it at the post office on our way to McDonald Inn. I haven't forgotten my promise to take you girls there."

Henny let out a tiny sigh. Grandma was at it again. Then what Grandpa had told her came into her head: Tell her. Tell her you need some time for yourself. Henny gave a little resolute bob of her chin. I'm brave, she said to herself. I wrote to Ellis, didn't I? I'm brave enough to talk to Grandma. She opened her mouth to speak, but nothing came out.

"Why don't you go call your sisters. They're out in the garden. I'll just go get my purse, and then we can leave." Grandma turned and left the kitchen.

Henny let out a much larger sigh.

"One more week to go," Alex practically sang as she came into the bedroom from brushing her teeth one morning.

Henny didn't reply. Four days had gone by since she'd sent her letter to Ellis, and she still hadn't said anything to Grandma. She was disgusted with herself.

"I don't want to go home," said Celia.

"What?" said Alex, staring at her younger sister. "Are you kidding? You tried to run away from here a few weeks ago."

"I know. But I don't want to anymore."

"Don't you want to see Mom and Dad?"

"Of course I do," said Celia. "But I want them to come here."

"Here? Why?"

"So we can keep on having The Lightey Club."

"We can have The Lightey Club at home."

Celia shook her head. "Lightey lives here." She refused to believe the lightning bugs were almost gone, no matter what Ellis had said (or even what she saw). "Right, Henny?"

Henny blinked. She hadn't been paying much

attention to her sisters' conversation. "What?" she asked.

"Doesn't Lightey live here?"

"Sure," she said.

Alex clucked her tongue. "It doesn't matter where he lives. We can have meetings anywhere. Can't we, Henny?"

"Lightey's immortal," Henny said, almost to herself.

"What?" asked Alex.

But Henny didn't answer her.

"You haven't even been listening," Alex said.

"And I like Grandpa," Celia said, completing a thought she'd had five minutes before. "Don't you, Alex?"

"Grandpa's okay," Alex answered gruffly. She didn't want to admit she liked him, too. "But Grandma isn't."

"Grandma doesn't mean to be a problem. She could be okay if . . ." Henny began.

"If what?"

If I talked with her, Henny thought, but she didn't tell Alex that. She just shrugged.

"Don't tell me you don't want to go home, either," Alex sneered.

"I do, but . . ." But I've got to take care of what Dad calls some "unfinished business" first, she thought.

"But what?"

Henny shrugged again.

Alex rolled her eyes. "You two are weird," she said.

"I am not," protested Celia.

But Henny didn't bother to disagree with her.

"Now, don't forget, Ed," Grandma said later that day. Her voice sounded tense to Henny. In fact, Grandma had seemed tense quite a bit lately. "You and the girls come over to Evelyn's at four o'clock. That's when we're having punch and cookies to honor the new president."

"Stella, it's your club meeting. I think we'll be out of place there."

"No, you won't. You're the new president's family."

"Stella," Grandpa said as kindly as he could. "You haven't been elected yet."

"That's true," Grandma said. "But Evelyn thinks I'm a shoo-in. Besides, even if I don't get elected, there's nothing wrong with my family showing up for some refreshments."

"All right, Stella," Grandpa said.

Henny wondered why Grandpa didn't tell her he didn't want to go, the way he'd advised her to do. Maybe he's trying to "be reasonable," she thought. "Good luck, Grandma," she said, and meant it.

Grandma smiled at her. "Thank you, Henny."

"Well, girls, what would you like to do today?" Grandpa asked them when Grandma had gone.

"The Lightey Club!" Celia yelled.

"Baseball," said Alex.

"Working in the garden?" suggested Henny.

"Why not all three?" asked Grandpa.

"Can we?" said Henny.

"Well, baseball might be pushing it a little. We could work in the garden and then have a Lightey Club meeting, though."

They all looked at Alex. "Okay," she said slowly. "I'll work in the garden—if you let me use the hose."

"You will be our official waterer," Grandpa told her.

"What official am I?" asked Celia.

"How about official galinsoga weeder."

"Huh?"

"See this plant with the little white flowers? I want you to pull it up."

"Pull it up? How come?"

"It's a weed, and it's going to choke out that pretty daisy over here."

"Oh. Okay," Celia said. She bent down and, with the tip of her tongue poking out of her mouth, she gave a grunt and pulled up the plant.

"Good going, Celia. Now, look at this plant carefully. Then go around the garden and pull up every plant just like it. If you're not sure it's just like it, ask me."

"Okay, Grandpa."

"What weeds do you want me to pull, Grandpa?" Henny asked.

"This stuff. Crabgrass."

"When do I start watering?" Alex asked.

"Later on. Want to pull some weeds first?"

"Sure."

"You can work with Henny. There's enough crabgrass to go around."

Then they all went to work. They moved steadily down the garden (except for Celia, who skipped from one spot to another) until their knees got so stiff they could hardly stand up.

"Whew," said Alex. "Is it watering time yet?"

"Yep. And lemonade time, too. I think I'll go fix some. Then we can have our meeting."

"Do we have enough time for it, Grandpa? Before we have to go meet Grandma, I mean," Henny asked.

Grandpa looked at his watch. "We have one hour, six minutes and thirty-two seconds. Think that's enough time?"

Henny nodded.

Grandpa unfurled the hose for Alex. "Let's see if you know how to water."

"Of course I know how to water. Everybody knows how to water," she said.

"Let's see," Grandpa insisted.

Alex took the hose from him and held it out over a plant.

"Uh-uh," he said. "That's not right. Do it this way to give the roots a good soaking." He took the hose from her and demonstrated. Then he handed it back to Alex.

"Like this?" she asked.

"Pretty good. Keep it up. I'll get that lemonade."

He went into the house.

Alex had been watering for a few minutes when Celia went over to her and said, "Now it's my turn."

"No it isn't. I'm the official waterer."

"You can be the official goslowga weeder." Celia grabbed for the hose.

Alex grabbed it back. They wrestled. The hose fell to the ground, nozzle up, spraying water all over both of them.

"Ahhhh!" they both squealed.

Henny started to laugh.

Alex picked up the hose and doused Henny. She squealed, too. Then she jumped up, plucked the hose out of Alex's hand, and sprayed her back.

"Fresh lemonade," Grandpa called.

Immediately, Henny gave the hose back to Alex, who started watering an already soggy batch of bell-flowers.

In another moment, Grandpa appeared with a tray on which were a pitcher and four glasses. He set the tray down on a small table. "Good work, Alex," he said. He didn't seem to notice that the three girls were all dripping wet.

"Wait, you missed a spot," he said, taking the hose from her.

"Where?" asked Alex.

"Here!" he said, and whipping around, he sprayed her right in the face.

"Mmmfff," said Alex. And, next thing, she got hold of the hose and sprayed Grandpa back.

Henny and Celia were doubled over laughing —

especially at the shocked expression on Alex's face. But when Alex noticed that Grandpa was laughing, too, she began to giggle.

All four of them were hysterical when Grandma appeared, her lips drawn in a thin line. She took in their wet clothes, and her lips grew even tighter.

"Stella!" Grandpa said. "What are you doing here?"

"Grandma, did you win?" asked Henny.

But Grandma didn't answer her.

"What do you think I'm doing here? It's five-thirty. The meeting's been over for an hour."

"Five-thirty. That's impossible. It's only . . ." Grandpa looked at his watch. Then he tapped it. "Uh-oh. It's stopped. Sorry, Stella."

"Sorry, sorry. Everyone's sorry!" Grandma spit out.

Everyone stared at her, stunned. Grandma *never* raised her voice like that.

"I've tried so hard with you girls this summer. So hard!" she cried. Then she turned and ran into the house.

Nobody could move. And it was a long moment before anyone could speak. Then Alex broke the silence. "I guess she lost," she said.

Chapter 10

Grandma?" Henny rapped on the door to her grandparents' bedroom. "Grandma, may I come in?"

"All right," came Grandma's voice, sounding rather distant.

Henny opened the door and went in. Grandma was lying on her bed, her head propped up by two pillows.

"Do you have another headache, Grandma?" Henny asked.

"No, I just feel . . . tired."

There was a pause. Then Henny said, "Grandma, I'm really sor—I mean, it's too bad you lost the election."

"Evelyn Lattislaw will make a very good president," Grandma said, too enthusiastically.

"Evelyn? I thought she told you . . ." Henny began. Then she stopped. Grandma didn't need to be reminded that her friend had misled her. "We didn't mean to miss the refreshments," Henny finished.

Another pause, and Grandma said, "I know you didn't, dear. I apologize for losing my temper. I don't know what came over me."

Henny was silent, so Grandma went on, "It has been a bit difficult, though, what with Celia running away and Alex being so resentful and then the business with Ellis. I wanted so much for you girls to enjoy yourselves. I wanted this to be your best visit ever. But six weeks is an awfully long time. I expected some problems at first. But the problems haven't really gone away. Alex is still resentful. Celia still misses your parents. And you, well, how do you feel, Henny?"

It was the first time Grandma had ever asked Henny that question that way. And all of a sudden, Henny wasn't afraid anymore of telling her. Her words came out in a rush. "This could've been the best visit ever, Grandma. I like this house. I love the garden. And I like going places with you, too—sometimes. But not all the time. That's how Alex and Celia feel, too. We're kids, Grandma. Kids have got to have time alone—just like grown-ups."

Grandma looked confused. "But . . . but . . . I was afraid you'd be bored. . . ." Her voice trailed off.

"We wouldn't have been. There's always something for a kid to do," Henny said. "Take Alex—she's wanted to play baseball all summer. And Celia—she'd be happy just digging in the dirt. And me—I like to read and look at things and . . . and . . ." Henny stopped, feeling shy all of a sudden.

"And what else?" Grandma asked.

"And daydream," Henny said in a low voice.

After a long moment, Grandma said, "I used to daydream, too. At least I think I did. It's been a long time." She sounded very sad.

"You can do it again, Grandma," Henny said. "If you want to."

Grandma smiled at her. "You may be right. You're a pretty smart kid."

Henny smiled back. "I'll let you rest now," she said, and walked out of the room. She hurried downstairs to the kitchen, where Alex and Celia were sitting. Grandpa had gone out for a walk.

"We've got to have a Lightey Club meeting," Henny said with determination, "to vote on another new member."

Celia looked puzzled, but Alex said, "Who? Wait a minute, you couldn't mean . . ."

"Uh-huh." Henny firmly nodded her head. "Grandma."

"Forget it, Henny."

"She's different now. She's not going to make us do all sorts of stuff with her all day long."

"I'll bet."

"It's true. And, besides, Lightey will help make sure she doesn't."

"How will he do that?" Alex asked.

"I don't know," said Henny. "I just know he will. Anyway, if I'm wrong, we only have one more week to go here, and we can stick that out."

"Grandma will like Lightey," Celia said. "Everybody does. Even Ms. Mantis. And Grandma's a lot like her."

Alex and Henny both stared at Celia, and, realizing she was right, they burst out laughing.

All five members of The Lightey Club were present and accounted for in the Geffens' garden. The bench and chairs were filled to capacity.

"We can't have any more members," said Celia.

"Why not?" asked Grandpa.

"We don't have any more seats."

"Oh, I think we could fix that—if anybody else wants to join," Grandma said.

"They can't want to join. We have to want them to," said Alex.

"Excuse me," said Grandma humbly. "You're absolutely right. I'm new and I don't know all the rules."

"You'll learn them, Grandma," said Celia.

"Are we ready to begin?" asked Henny.

"Ready!" everyone sang out.

"Are you ready, Henny?" teased Grandpa.

"Yes."

"Then begin!" shouted Alex and Celia.

"All right," said Henny.

o o o

It was dusk, and all the bugs were excited. In a few minutes the contest would begin. The three finalists, who had already been chosen, would get their chance to tell a story and try for the title of Speaker of the House and Garden. The rules, approved by Ms. Mantis, chief judge, were (1) the story had to be true; (2) it had to be a personal account; (3) it had to be full of admirable values.

The crowd had been gathering for some time at the leaf that was a stage, and they were already growing restless and noisy. But the minute Ms. Mantis entered, the buzzing stopped. Accompanying her were the three other judges she had selected — Millicent Ladybug, Ms. Mantis's assistant and secretary of the Society for the Improvement of the Beetle Image; Nick the Fly with an Eye for News; and Clover Honeybee, the hard-working, respectable, and well-liked chief worker of the bees.

"I am pleased to see such a wonderful turnout," Ms. Mantis addressed the crowd. "I know you will not be disappointed by the stories that are to follow. Without delay, let me introduce our judges." And she did. "Now, Clover Honeybee would like to make a brief and happy announcement."

The bee leaped to her wings and buzzed, "I just want to say that Her Highness Honeybee, our beloved Queen, has had two thousand, two hundred, and forty-three children hatch today, and they are all healthy."

"Hooray," the bugs yelled.

"Yes. And, although unfortunately she couldn't attend tonight's contest, she sends her love and best wishes."

"Three cheers for the Queen," yelled a boisterous bumblebee in the audience. And everyone cheered.

"Now, please give your attention to Gloria the Garden Spider, our first finalist."

Out crawled Gloria and, in her typically straightforward manner, she immediately began to speak. "This is about my first web. I discovered that I could spin, and that changed my life. I almost fell off a twig, you see, but I didn't, because this thread automatically came out of me and suspended me from the twig. What's this, I thought to myself, and then I found out. I was born to be an artist. All my webs have been perfect. If the wind rips one, I don't worry too much. I just fix it or start another. But back to my first web. I started with a . . . weblike structure and I took one strand and . . ."

The audience tried to be polite but was having a lot of trouble.

"She's a good spider, but she's so boring," Franny the Young Firefly whispered to Jerome the Firefly.

"She can't help it. Spiders are terrible speakers."

"Then I put the fiftieth strand in place. Then I put the fifty-first strand in place . . ."

"Why'd they let her speak, then?"

"'Cause her story is (1) true; (2) personal; (3) full of admirable values."

"Oh."

"So I keep doing that and pretty soon I have a sturdy web. I use it as a home and a trap for flies and things I eat. It's also really pretty in the spring and summer mornings with dew on it. That's when I really know I'm an artist . . ."

The bugs were humming louder, wriggling, fluttering, and buzzing in their places.

"Her speech is a flop. I wish she would stop," mumbled George the Centipede.

"Yeah, they should've made you a finalist, eh, George. You wouldn't have bored 'em. Ha, ha," boomed Morris the Earthworm.

"Morris, you bore us." The centipede yawned.

"I'm insulted. The worm burns. Ha, ha."

"My latest web was constructed the same way as my first web. First, I take one strand and I attach it. Then I . . ."

"Enough already! Quit it!" yelled a loud waterbug.

"Yeah, next speech," a wasp bellowed.

"Stop that bellowing immediately," Ms. Mantis said.

"Never mind," Gloria said sadly. "No one appreciates art anymore. No one has any time." And she crawled off.

"There is a distinct lack of manners in this assembly," Millicent said.

"Millicent, I'll talk to Gloria after the contest, but

we must continue," Ms. Mantis said. "Our second finalist is Twinky the Monarch Butterfly."

"Lightey, I can't do it yet. Please go before me," Twinky whispered.

"Sure, Twink, sure — if Ms. Mantis will let me." So Lightey, hoping he was unnoticed, flew to Nick and told him to pass the message to Ms. Mantis.

"Excuse me, but there will be a slight change in the order of speaking," Ms. Mantis said. "Lightey the Lightning Bug will be our next speaker, followed by Twinky the Monarch Butterfly."

Lightey had felt confident enough until he actually got on the leaf-stage and faced the audience. "Uh . . . Ms. Mantis . . . uh . . . has requested me to talk about how I became . . . uh . . . well . . . kind of . . . what you might call . . . the . . . uh . . . Aw, gee . . . I can't call myself that, Ms. Mantis. . . . Okay, the Top Bug."

"You sure are, Lightey, and a good one, too," Franny yelled loudly.

"Yay, Lightey," the others cheered.

"Thanks, but shut up, will ya," he said. "Anyway, I would say my family helped a lot — in my becoming a leader, that is. My great-grandmother was from Japan, and she taught my grandparents, who taught my parents, who taught me that the Japanese people believed that we — fireflies, that is — are the spirits of warriors, and my grandmother said we should live up to that. My grandfather allowed scientists to study his light." At that, Lightey glowed proudly.

"Hooray," cheered Franny.

"Big deal," said the boisterous bumblebee.

"And my parents were good bugs who encouraged me. When I came here, all the fireflies were getting a rotten deal. I mean, nobody was paying any attention to them 'cause they were disorganized. So I, uh, organized them."

"You said it!" Franny yelled.

"Disorganized!" sniffed another lightning bug.

"Who cares?" said the bumblebee.

"Yeah, they were really doing nothing, so I just called a few meetings. I started the weekly Firefly Display series and the monthly Meet Your Mate parties. I insisted on regular attendance. I called rehearsals . . ." Lightey was beginning to enjoy his speech.

"What does he mean, we were doing nothing?" a firefly said.

"It's true . . ." Jerome began.

But the other bugs drowned him out with grumbles.

"I really got us into shape. I got things done. I worked them hard. They were pretty darn lazy, and it took all my qualities of leadership to get them off their stomachs . . ."

The grumbling grew louder.

"This is too much," said one bug.

"Who does he think he is," said another.

"He's swell," piped a supporter.

"Yeah, swell-headed," replied the bumblebee.

"I had to be tough. I had to be brave. I had to use

my brains, my wings, my antennae, my heart, and my light. A bug's got to do what a bug's got to do. And I had to become a leader."

The grumbling rose. Everyone was talking at once. "He is . . ." "He's not . . ." "He is . . ." "He's not . . ."

"In fact, if I hadn't come . . ."

"Throw the bum out," yelled the bumblebee.

"Want to fight?" said Jerome.

Shouts rang out. "Cut it, Lightey." "What about us?" "Give it to 'em." "Who do you think you are." "You show 'em." The noise reached such a pitch that Lightey was forced to notice.

"Uh, well, they're good bugs. The best in the world. And everything worked out, as you can see. And I'm proud to work with them." Lightey finished abruptly and fled the stage.

But the hubbub continued.

"The conceit of that bug," Millicent muttered to Oliver Stag Beetle.

"Yes, I always thought his head was too big for his shell."

"No pre-judging, please," Ms. Mantis said politely and firmly to them. "The next and last finalist is Twinky the Monarch Butterfly."

"Lots of luck, Twink," Lightey whispered as he passed. "I think I got carried away."

"Oh, no, you were great," said Twinky, who was so nervous she hadn't heard a word of his story. "Lightey, stay with me."

"Twink, you're on now."

"I can't do it."

"Oh, yes, you can." And with that, he gave her a shove.

She fluttered off balance to the leaf-stage, alighted, and flew off again.

"Our next speaker is Twinky the Monarch Butterfly," Ms. Mantis repeated.

Again Twinky approached the leaf-stage and turned back. Fortunately, only the judges noticed because the crowd was still busy debating Lightey's speech.

With Lightey's encouragement, Twinky tried once again and succeeded in landing and remaining on the platform.

"Before I came to the Geffens' garden, when I was still a little caterpillar," she began in a tiny voice, "my mother told me I'd never have to be afraid of birds when I grew up. In fact, my mother said, 'The only thing you'll have to watch out for are humans with nets.' "

"He thinks he's so great," sneered an ant whose picnic plans had been thwarted by Lightey.

"He *is* great. Everything he said is true," Franny yelled back.

No one was listening to Twinky, but she had started speaking and couldn't stop.

" 'What do humans do, Mama?' I asked.

" 'They sneak up on you, scoop you up, put you in a jar where you choke and die, and then they pin you in a case, near a lot of other victims. That's what happened to your Aunt Emily,' she answered.

"'But why do they do that, Mama?' I asked, terrified.

"'Because . . .' she paused.

"'Why?' I insisted.

"'Because they think it's scientific. And, also, they like to collect pretty things,' she answered."

"All right, so he got a little carried away, but that's because he's embarrassed by his greatness," Jerome argued.

"Greatness, my antennae, he's just had good luck," snorted a small moth.

"You wouldn't know greatness if you smashed into it," Jerome snapped back.

". . . snug in my chrysalis. I kept thinking about my mother's words, but I didn't understand the business about birds." Twinky's voice was growing louder and more confident, but she was still unaware that no one was listening. "One day, I felt strange stirrings in my body, and at first I was frightened, but then I realized what was happening — my mother had explained it all beforehand. I worked my way out of the chrysalis. It took ages. Finally, damp and weak, I entered the sunlight. My wings were funny-looking, I remember, wrinkled and shrunken. I couldn't do anything but rest and dry out."

"I could've made a better speech than that lightning bug's," a pushy cricket chirped.

"Sure you could've, if Ms. Mantis had written it for you. And, even then, I'm not so sure," a grasshopper who admired Lightey chirped in return.

It was then that Ms. Mantis, realizing that poor Twinky was speaking to no one but the judges, angrily turned to the audience.

"Silence, invertebrates," she boomed so extraordinarily loudly that everyone jumped and stopped talking immediately.

No one had the faintest idea what she meant, but it sounded bad enough.

"'Ugh,' he rasped, and flew off, not hurting me at all. I thought he was very rude." Twinky's voice floated above the silence. "Later, when I was strong enough to fly, I went for a snack at a nearby milkweed. While I was sipping, something grabbed one of my wings.

"'Ptooey.' This very young thrush spit. You know what she said? She said, 'What is this? Gotta get me a snail quick to get that taste outta my mouth.' How do you like that? I thought it was a close call and examined myself for cuts and bruises. I wasn't hurt, but I was really upset, and I wondered what was wrong with me."

"Please remain quiet and listen to the rest of Twinky's story," Ms. Mantis said unnecessarily, for the crowd was terribly quiet.

"Then I met this little white butterfly. Her name is Angel, and she became my best friend. She asked if I were okay, and we talked about our names. She hated hers, and I told her mine is really Twinkassimar, after my great-grandmother. I bet you all didn't

know that. Ha, ha." Twinky had memorized her speech, jokes and all, so thoroughly that she not only didn't leave out a line of it, but she couldn't.

"So I asked her, 'Why don't the birds eat me?'

"'You mean your mama never told you?' she answered. 'You're a monarch, that's why. Birds don't eat royalty.' She was too polite to tell me how awful I taste. Our conversation was interrupted by the sound of wings.

"'It's a blue jay. I'm a goner,' Angel squeaked.

"Then I did something which surprised me. I said, 'Oh, no, you're not. Flatten your wings and lie still.' And I perched on top of her and spread my wings over her.

"'Ugh! You again! I thought I saw a tasty little cabbage butterfly somewhere around here. I must have my eyes checked by Marsh Hawk,' that awful blue jay said, and flew away."

The audience was caught up by Twinky's speech. Twinky was caught up with it, too, and was changing her voice to suit the different characters in it.

"'Did I crush you, Angel?' I said.

"'Crush me? You saved me! Twinky, you saved me!' Angel yelled.

"'Royalty must always protect its subjects,' I joked.

"Then Angel promised that if I ever needed it, she'd do the same for me. Little did she know that she'd have to live up to those words sooner than she expected. The very next morning I woke up with the sun and was happy to be alive. I wondered where Angel was and if we could have breakfast together. The next thing I knew, Angel and three of her friends were fluttering next to me. 'Don't move. A human with a net,' she said. I trembled. She ordered me once more to be still. Then, all four butterflies covered me.

"A breathless boy ran into the garden to my milkweed, but all he saw were a bunch of white butterflies. I heard him say, 'Phooey, common old cabbage butterflies. The monarch must've flown off. It would've looked really pretty next to my swallowtail.' And then he went back into his house.

"We all shook ourselves. Angel told me she had been near the window and had seen the boy pulling a net out of his closet; she had seen him use the net only once before, but she had never forgotten it. Angel and I have been friends ever since we saved each other, and we visit each other whenever we can."

Twinky stopped dead. Her story was finished. She gave a little shake and realized she was onstage and facing an audience. "Oh, hello . . . I'm Twinky. . . . My story . . . Before I came to the Geffens' garden . . . Before . . . before . . . oh, dear." And, embarrassed and dizzy, she rushed off the stage.

The audience giggled and then broke into laughter, confusing and embarrassing the poor butterfly even more. She flew so rapidly and blindly, she crashed into Lightey.

"Hey, Twink, I didn't know you were so talented," he said, after recovering from the impact.

"Whaat?" Twinky asked.

"Your speech. It was great—especially for a bug with no experience. I've spoken a lot, as you know, but you haven't—and you sure can."

"What speech?" Twinky stared at Lightey.

"Come off it, Twinky. Enough's enough. I'm your friend."

"What speech?"

"Look, if you're making fun—"

But Lightey was interrupted by Ms. Mantis. "We judges have made our decision. The title of Speaker of the House and Garden is awarded to—Twinky the Monarch Butterfly."

A great cheer rose, and everyone called for Twinky.

"You did it, Twink," said Lightey. "Of course, I'll give you some pointers for your next one."

"My next what?"

"Sheesh," said Lightey, just as the audience stormed the stage and carried Twinky off around the garden. Shouts filled the air: "Brilliant!" "Glorious." "Moving." "One of the Year's Ten Best." "Dazzling!" "Will you marry me?" Everyone was ecstatic—everyone, that is, except Twinky, who had no idea of what she'd done. Strangely enough, afterward, no matter how often she was told, she still never remembered. But every month when, in her capacity of Speaker of the House and Garden, she had to make a speech, she repeated, word for word, the story that had won her the title. And each time,